He frowned and stroked his chin with a finger as if deep in thought.

Iris waited a moment or two for him to answer. She had opened her mouth to ask him again when he dropped his hand and nodded at her.

"Lance Sherer. Nice man. Very smart. He already has a wife, y'know. And children." He hiccuped and smiled at her. A dimple appeared in his left cheek, making him appear debonair in spite of the wrinkled condition of his dark suit.

"Well, I never!" Her indignation made her splutter the words. What was the man thinking? "I am a good friend of his wife. I've come at her suggestion."

"Is there a problem here?" Unnoticed, another man had stepped through the doors of the tavern.

Foreboding made Iris's heart thump loudly. Now she faced two strangers, and both of them were likely inebriated.

DIANE ASHLEY, a "town girl" born and raised in Mississippi, has worked more than twenty years for the House of Representatives. She rediscovered a thirst for writing, was led to a class taught by Aaron McCarver, and became a founding member of the Bards of Faith. Visit her at www.bardsoffaith.homestead.com

AARON McCARVER is a transplanted Mississippian who was raised in the mountains near Dunlap, Tennessee. He loves his jobs of teaching at two Christian colleges and editing for Barbour Publishing. A member of ACFW, he is coauthor with Gilbert Morris of the bestselling series, The Spirit of Appalachia.

Books by Diane Ashley and Aaron McCarver

HEARTSONG PRESENTS
HP860—Under the Tulip Poplar

Don't miss out on any of our super romances. Write to us at the following address for information on our newest releases and club information.

Heartsong Presents Readers' Service
PO Box 721
Uhrichsville, OH 44683

Or visit www.heartsongpresents.com

A Bouquet for Iris

Diane Ashley and Aaron McCarver

Heartsong Presents

To our fellow Bards of Faith. You are more than just critique partners. You are friends and family. We have shared so many things. . .both good and bad. Thank you for always being there through it all. We look forward to sharing many more special times together—including your many future contracts! God bless us all as we continue to write for Him.

A note from the Authors:
We love to hear from our readers! You may correspond with us by writing:

Diane Ashley and Aaron McCarver
Author Relations
PO Box 721
Uhrichsville, OH 44683

ISBN 978-1-60260-675-3

A BOUQUET FOR IRIS

All scripture quotations are taken from the King James Version of the Bible.

All of the characters and events in this book are fictitious. Any resemblance to actual persons, living or dead, or to actual events is purely coincidental.

Our mission is to publish and distribute inspirational products offering exceptional value and biblical encouragement to the masses.

PRINTED IN THE U.S.A.

one

Iris Landon bunched the soft velvet of her new gown into gloved hands as she descended from the family carriage and followed her parents up the steps to Aunt Dolly and Uncle Mac's home. Most ladies her age would be excited about the evening's festivities, but she rather dreaded them.

This was not the first of Aunt Dolly's Christmas Eve galas she had attended, and she knew what lay ahead. She would have to sit through a long dinner, listening to the latest gossip about the elite families of Nashville. There would also be the obligatory inquiries about her plans to marry. Iris had learned over the past year to smile and nod as various relatives offered advice on how to attract the interest of the young gentlemen of the area.

Eventually everyone would move to the ballroom, and she would be forced to spend hours listening to endless chatter from other young ladies when she'd much rather be discussing westward expansion or the plight of the Indian nations. She would endure the usual games, and at least one of the more enterprising young men would seek to steal a kiss from his dancing partner by maneuvering her underneath a sprig of mistletoe while it still held kissing berries. She had half a mind to pull off the berries herself just to make sure no one tried anything that silly with her.

Iris lifted her gaze to the clear night sky, and her breath

caught. Against the horizon, a single star rose, and for a moment she was transported to the days of Matthew's Gospel. What a miraculous sight the star must have been on the night Christ was born. Had the wise men been weary when they arrived in Bethlehem? Or had their anticipation wiped out all the long, fearsome months of travel? She closed her eyes for a moment as the creak of a harness was transformed into noises from burdened camels. Golden light pressed against her eyelids like the torchlight from inside Mary and Joseph's humble home. Her flight of fancy ended when the opening of the front door and her great-aunt's greeting brought her back to the present.

Aunt Dolly practically glowed in the light pouring out of her foyer. She wore a rose-colored dress with crimson piping and a scattering of decorative gold bows. She might be diminutive, but from the peacock feathers perched atop her graying hair to the tips of her shiny black slippers, Aunt Dolly looked as regal as European royalty.

"Rebekah, you become more beautiful every year, dearest." What Aunt Dolly lacked in height, she made up for with enthusiasm, catching Iris's mother in a warm hug before turning to her father. "And Asher, don't you look as distinguished as ever. I'll never understand why you didn't stay with President Jackson. He certainly needs better advisers—someone to convince him that the poor Indians shouldn't be forced out of their homes."

The others might not have noticed, but Iris saw her father grimace slightly at Aunt Dolly's remark before he bowed over her hand. "I doubt anyone could change the president's mind once he has made a decision. The only person who might have done that is no longer with us."

Aunt Dolly sighed. "I really miss Rachel, too. Not only was she a gentling influence on her husband, she was one of my dearest friends." She shook her head as if to clear it of gloomy thoughts before turning to the tall man who hovered in the hallway behind her. "Look who has arrived, Mac. It's the Landons."

"So I see." Robert "Mac" McGhee raised Ma's gloved hand to his lips. He always made Iris think of a wrestler, with his widespread stance and thick chest. He didn't look very comfortable in starched trousers and a long-tailed coat. He straightened, and she noticed that the collar of his shirt was already beginning to droop a little, as though he'd been tugging at it before their arrival.

As he turned toward her father, Iris saw the glint of his pistol handle peeking underneath his coat. She wondered if Aunt Dolly realized that her husband, the retired sheriff of Davidson County, was armed.

"Iris, child, come here so I can see you." Aunt Dolly pulled her forward into the pool of light thrown by dozens of candles in the foyer. "I declare, you've grown a foot since I saw you last."

Uncle Mac tossed a wink at her. Trust the dear man to bolster her confidence. He was one of the few men who stood head and shoulders taller than she and therefore knew how awkward it felt to tower over others. He bent to kiss her cheek and helped her remove her brown wool cloak. Glad to be relieved of its weight in the warm house, Iris shook out the folds of her skirt.

"Whatever were you thinking, dressing your daughter in lavender, Rebekah?" Aunt Dolly's voice practically quivered with dismay as she caught sight of Iris's new gown. "All the young men I've invited will think she's in mourning."

Iris wanted to roll her eyes but kept her gaze firmly fixed on the floor. She did not want to embarrass her parents by showing disrespect toward her aunt. She refused to believe, however, that her choice of dress color was important to anyone but her.

"You know how our Iris loves shades of purple." Ma unbuttoned her black cloak and slipped it off her shoulders, bringing into view the golden brocade dress that reflected the rich color of her hair. The generous skirt swirled around her ankles as she handed the wrap to Uncle Mac before turning back to Aunt Dolly. "I blame it on her father, who insisted we name her after his favorite flower."

"Besides, Aunt Dolly, no matter what color I chose, it would not make me appear even one inch shorter." Iris swept one long arm in a downward arc. "Most men in attendance will want to avoid dancing with a beanpole."

Uncle Mac handed their cloaks and coats to the house-keeper. "Now Iris, don't be foolish. I'm sure all the young lads will think you are the most delightful girl in the room."

Aunt Dolly sputtered for a moment. "Men! You never understand fashion."

Iris's father cocked an eyebrow at Aunt Dolly. "I believe you have won Mac's argument for him. If men have no clue about fashion, then you need not worry yourself about the color or style of Iris's dress."

Iris held her breath, fully expecting her volatile aunt to launch into a diatribe about the fundamental importance of fashion and color. She wished for a moment that she had let Ma talk her into purchasing the bolt of green material the storekeeper had said would bring out the highlights in Iris's brown eyes. But she had never really liked the color green, except perhaps in springtime. And then only because it meant her flower namesake would soon be in bloom.

Every year since she was about five, she had waited impatiently for the irises in Ma's flower garden to begin showing their colors. Some would be dark and velvety like the night sky, while others bloomed a pale color reminiscent of early morning or late evening. The latter were her favorite blossoms and the reason she'd chosen the material for her new dress.

And why shouldn't she choose to please her own taste? None of tonight's guests were likely to go into a decline when they saw she was not wearing white or some other insipid color. It wasn't as if she would be inundated with dance partners no matter what color she chose.

As she had pointed out to Aunt Dolly, she was much too tall. And it seemed that she would never stop growing. The last time Pa measured, her height was a full eight inches above five feet. When one added her inability to make light, flirtatious conversation, the result was abysmal.

Not the type to simper mindlessly, Iris wanted to debate political issues like the discovery of gold on Indian lands, the abolition of slavery, or even popular literature or classic poetry. It seemed that most men preferred giggling, empty-headed girls. And if that's what they wanted, then she didn't want them.

Aunt Dolly stomped her foot. "I should have known all of you would join forces against me." She held her frown for an instant longer before dissolving into laughter. "And why must you always be right?"

Uncle Mac's deep laugh harmonized with Aunt Dolly's delicate notes. "I know better than to answer a question like that." He shook a finger at her. "Almost two decades with you has taught me when to agree with my adorable wife."

Aunt Dolly's ire seemingly melted completely away. She unfolded a lace-edged rose fan and tapped her husband's arm with it. "You are indeed a very smart man."

Ma nodded her agreement before turning to Pa. "Asher, while I appreciate your defense of masculine logic, you really should not encourage our daughter to rebel against fashionable dictates."

He bowed before holding out both elbows, one for his wife and one for his daughter. "I'm certain all the young men will pay enough attention to Iris to satisfy your dreams and raise my misgivings."

Iris forced her lips into a smile although she wanted to groan as they made their way to the dining room. This was a familiar point of contention for her parents. Pa was willing to let her wait until God led the right man into her life, but Ma was anxious for her to marry and settle down nearby. It wasn't as though she didn't want to marry and start a family. What girl wouldn't? But she knew that a marriage without God's blessing was a recipe for disaster.

And she had a good idea of the kind of man whom God would send. He would appreciate her unique strengths instead of expecting her to be an imitation of every other girl in the area. He would love her like Pa loved Ma. Until God led someone like Pa into her life, she was more than willing to wait.

Iris was not sure she wanted to live in Nashville for the rest of her life either. Didn't Ma realize what a big world was out there to be explored? There were so many towns and settlements nowadays and people passing through the area in search of land to the west of the Mississippi River. It was not fair that single women could not join a wagon train. Iris was fully capable of taking care of herself. She had no need of a man to help her drive a wagon or fix dinner. If only she could explore the country and see for herself all the land beyond the Mississippi River. The newspapers promised land enough for all, white and Indians alike.

Some nights after all of her family had gone to bed, Iris would sit at the window in her bedroom and search the horizon for answers. She wasn't even sure what the questions were, only that God had placed in her heart the desire to leave Nashville and search for a different kind of life.

Iris stood to one side as Pa helped her ma to her seat. Her gaze drank in the long table covered with pine greenery, holly berries, and silver serving dishes. Flickering candlelight from the large chandelier hanging over the center of the table gilded the edges of the delicate china place settings. Not only was Aunt Dolly a fashion plate, she knew how to create a wonderful atmosphere in her lovely home. Even with her limited interest in such things, Iris could appreciate the artistry of the formal dining room.

When they were all seated, Uncle Mac leaned forward and closed his eyes. Iris followed his lead and listened as he blessed the food, the arrival of loved ones, and the celebration of Christ's birth.

Warmth seeped through her at the thought of Baby Jesus being born. What a miraculous event that reached out to envelop all of them this evening. She added her thanks to having been raised in a Christian home. The good Lord had showered so many blessings on her and her family.

Uncle Mac ended the prayer, and Iris let her gaze drift around the table as her relatives talked about their plans for the Christmas season and the upcoming year. She could not repress a shiver of anticipation. Surely the Lord wouldn't wait much longer before showing her His plan for her life.

❧

Eugene Brown escorted Iris to a group of ladies who included her ma, Aunt Dolly, and Grandma Landon, her paternal grandmother. Iris thanked him for their dance and wondered if he realized how much relief showed on his face as he left her standing with her relatives.

Grandma Landon raised her brows at Eugene's abrupt

departure. "Someone ought to teach that young man his manners. He didn't even speak, much less thank my granddaughter for dancing with him."

Aunt Dolly nodded. "Young people these days have such lackadaisical habits."

"Perhaps we should not be so hasty to judge." Ma's voice gently chided the others as she turned and watched Eugene dash out of the ballroom. "You see, the poor boy may have a valid reason to hurry."

"He probably needs to go rub his feet." Iris could not keep the mischief out of her voice. "I know I must have stepped on them a dozen times during our dance."

All three of her relatives were taken aback by her pronouncement, but then Ma smiled. "I did notice that Mr. Brown was a bit shorter than you."

Iris raised her eyebrows. "His head was at the level of my shoulder. And his steps were so short I felt I was mincing my way through our dance."

Her grandmother studied her from head to toe. "You may be a bit tall, child, but that color you're wearing is very becoming."

A sound of irritation came from Aunt Dolly. "Doesn't anyone in this family have a bit of fashion consciousness?"

Grandma looked somewhat affronted at the comment, but she must have decided to exercise her manners by ignoring Aunt Dolly's question. She turned her attention to her daughter-in-law. "Where are your parents, Rebekah?"

"They volunteered to entertain Hannah and Eli this evening so they would not have to stay at the house alone."

"I'm surprised you didn't volunteer for that duty, given your oft-repeated disdain for parties."

"I wouldn't let her stay home this year," Aunt Dolly answered for Ma. "Of course, I was hoping she would bring the children with her."

Ma shuddered. "You don't know what you're asking."

Iris could feel the corners of her mouth turning up. "Our Eli has far too much energy to behave himself all evening. If he had come, you would all bemoan his inability to mind his manners."

A flurry of activity at the door gained their attention. Several footmen were bringing a shiny washtub into the ballroom. Aunt Dolly excused herself and moved toward them to supervise the placement of the tub. Iris knew from previous parties that it was filled nearly to the rim with water. The housekeeper entered with a sack of apples that she dumped into the tub as soon as Aunt Dolly was happy with its placement.

Iris clapped her hands together. "Can I try catching an apple this year, Ma?"

Grandma looked up at the ceiling as if for guidance before addressing Iris's mother. "I hope you will not allow any such thing, Rebekah. It's not seemly for a young lady to dampen her gown or hair by taking part in such high jinks."

"I have to agree, Iris." Ma reached out and tweaked one of her daughter's curls. "Your coiffure already seems to be in some danger of coming undone. You would not want to be seen with your hair around your shoulders."

Iris reached up and patted some errant strands back into place. It was a shame her naturally curly hair was so thick and heavy. Ma had spent nearly an hour taming her unruly mane this evening before they came to the party, but she could tell it was trying to escape the dozens of pins that had been twisted into it. "Perhaps I could take it down and plait it like I used to do?"

Ma looked as if she was considering the request, but then she shook her head. "You are a grown woman now, Iris. The time for you to sport braids in public is long gone."

Iris let her shoulders droop, but then an idea popped into

her head. "If I'm so grown, then won't you reconsider that advertisement in the *Sentinel*?"

"What advertisement?" Grandma asked. "And what are you doing reading newspapers? Does your ma not give you enough chores to fill your day?"

Ma tossed a warning look at Iris. "We have gone through this several times, dear. You know that your father and I prayed about your request. We simply don't think it is advisable for you to travel to some little town in the wilderness to teach youngsters."

"What?" Grandma's voice was so loud that several people looked in their direction. "This is exactly my point, Rebekah. Young girls should not be allowed to fill their minds with all types of information. It's not good for them. You see what can come of it. Now your daughter wants to travel all alone to some unknown destination."

"It's not unknown." Iris defended her position. "It's a town in Texas called Shady Gulch. Doesn't that sound like a wonderful destination? I can practically see the little schoolhouse standing in front of a field of wildflowers, all whitewashed and sparkling. And it would be so fulfilling to help mold young people's minds."

"Or be attacked by marauding Indians or the Mexican army." Her grandma shuddered. "Just because a town has a pretty name does not mean it's a desirable destination."

Ma patted Iris's hand. "I know you want to teach youngsters, but there are lots of opportunities to do so right here in Nashville."

"Quite right." Grandma smoothed the front of her blue-and-white-striped skirt. "Why would you want to leave your loved ones?"

Iris wanted to argue with them, but she knew better. The look in Ma's eyes was the same one she got when she had to chase a fox away from the chicken coop—determined. Iris sighed and turned to watch the young men who were taking turns trying to bite into one of the apples floating in the tub. Some of the young ladies had drifted in that direction to cheer for their favorite participants.

Eugene had come back in, and he was standing next to Melissa Baker, a young lady who was several inches shorter than he. It looked like she was trying to convince him to compete in the apple bobbing. But from the way he was shaking his head, Iris had the feeling he had no desire to accede to her wishes. Poor Eugene. It seemed that things were going from bad to worse for him this evening.

Pa walked over to them and put an arm around Ma's waist.

Ma looked up at him. "Aren't you going to bob for apples this year?"

Pa laughed. "I think it's time for me to retire and leave the horseplay to the younger generation."

The others talked about past Christmases, but Iris's thoughts turned down a different avenue. She wished her expectations had not been met this evening. It would have been nice if some tall, handsome stranger had appeared and whisked her onto the dance floor.

She could almost see him—dark and handsome and, oh, so tall. He would have a mustache and hair that fell just so across his forehead. He would whisper sweet compliments into her ear and make her feel graceful and beautiful. Then he would bring her back to her parents and spend time talking intelligently with them of current events and his passion to serve the Lord. After the evening was over, her parents would be equally impressed by him. Then, of course, he would ride out to the farm to see her every day this winter, regardless of the cold and snow. And then he would propose in the springtime—

"Iris?" Ma's voice intruded on her sweet imaginings. "Are you ready to leave, dear?"

Iris refocused her attention on her parents, surprised to see that Grandma Landon was no longer standing with them. The advanced hour seemed to hit her all at once. She covered a yawn with her hand.

Pa smiled at her. "It looks as if our daughter is more than ready. If we don't whisk her away soon, I'm concerned she will fall asleep standing in the foyer." He led them to the doorway where Aunt Dolly and Uncle Mac stood.

After hugs and best wishes were exchanged, Iris collected her cloak and followed her parents to the waiting carriage. Cold night air made her nose tingle, but the warm bricks at her feet kept her from shivering. She drifted in and out of sleep as her parents talked quietly of the evening. She heard her pa mention something about a meeting of the Cherokee leaders, but the words wove themselves into her dreams. Tomorrow she would remember to ask him about it.

two

Adam Stuart balled up his left fist and shook it at the dark sky, even though he cringed inwardly at the bleak hatred consuming his heart. But how could a caring God allow such a thing to happen?

Up until this day, he'd hoped he was wrong, but today he'd been proven absolutely correct in his pessimistic predictions. He spat at the ground. The treaty had been signed in New Echota this afternoon, a few days after Christmas. This should be a season of rejoicing and celebrating the human birth of God, not a time of fear and perfidy.

Today Adam had been an appalled witness to the worst kind of travesty. A small group of Cherokee leaders had sold their people's extensive landholdings in Georgia, Tennessee, North Carolina, and Alabama to officials of the United States. They had willingly agreed to abandon their homes, move their families hundreds of miles away to a wild and unforgiving wilderness, and start all over again.

Couldn't they see this would not be the end? They had been conceding tracts of their land to white men for more than two decades. And still they were asked to move—again and again and again. If this pattern continued, the Cherokee would soon be nothing more than a memory, a footnote in the history of the United States. Why had God created these people if He was willing to let them be destroyed? And why had God given Adam this desire to protect them?

Adam looked up once more at the sky. Hadn't he given up everything to pursue his mission? And for what? The bitter taste of absolute defeat.

A harsh laugh escaped his chapped lips. Loss and defeat were his only companions anymore. What would he say to those who were depending on him back in Ross's Landing? What would John Ross, the real leader of the Cherokee Nation, say? How could he justify what had happened? Would things look better tomorrow? Or worse?

Could he have done anything to change the treaty signing? His mind saw again the hard faces of the Cherokee and the gleeful expressions of the white officers. Both sides had already made up their minds and were not willing to listen to anything he said. He'd tried everything, hadn't he? No matter what arguments he put forth, no one wanted to admit the possibility of making a terrible mistake. In the absence of Chief Ross, why hadn't he been able to make John Ridge and his followers see that their actions would affect the Cherokee people for generations to come? Betrayed by these chieftains who actually represented only a small number of the tribe, what would they do?

The night seemed to grow even darker as Adam tried to make himself face the inevitable. The God he had always worshipped was apparently a white God who cared nothing for the plight of Indians, whether they worshipped Him or not. The Bible spoke of a God who loved and protected the helpless and innocent, but Adam had learned to disregard such fanciful stories.

His horse whinnied. Adam leaned forward, feeling a little guilty to have forced his faithful mount back onto the path they'd traveled that very afternoon. "Careful, Samson. I know you're cold, but you have great strength in these—"

Samson reared up, and Adam fought to keep his seat. What was wrong with his horse?

A moment later he realized that the shadows to his right were moving. It was the only warning he had. Suddenly he was surrounded by a silent, deadly group. He fought to reach his rifle, but it was hopeless.

A noiseless adversary threw himself toward the saddle.

Adam clung to the pommel with dogged determination, but a blow to his head made him see stars. He was jerked off Samson. He crashed to the ground and tasted the cold, wet soil of the path he'd been traveling. Still fighting, Adam turned over in time to see the edge of a tomahawk sweeping toward him. A mighty roll sent him off the path and into dense brush. Thorns caught at his clothing and tore at his skin.

Grunts and stomps followed him into the forest.

With no time to get to his feet, he kept rolling. And then he was free of the brambles, hurtling downward to what would likely be his last resting place.

❧

Something tickled Adam's nose. A leaf? He reached up to bat it away and groaned. His arm hurt. He squinted to focus his vision, surprised to see dappled sunlight sparkling on dew-laced grass. Where was he? The woods? That was odd. He tried to sit up, but pain pushed him back against the cold ground.

He took a deep breath and tried to remember what had happened. He'd been going back home. Then he remembered his restive horse and moving shadows. He'd been attacked! His outspokenness at the treaty signing must have caused some in the Ridge party to think he was a liability.

Adam remembered falling under the blows and rolling away from his attackers. They must have left him for dead. Adam realized he was lucky to be alive, but his luck was going to run out if he couldn't find his way to shelter.

He decided to try rolling over. The pain was excruciating. He clamped his lips against the yell filling his chest. His assailants might still be in the area. He managed to get one elbow under him then the other. The effort had his body slick with sweat even though Adam could feel cold air against his skin.

He pushed against his elbows and managed to get his head and upper torso high enough to look around him. Wilderness was all he saw. He could hear a nearby stream, which made him realize how parched his throat was. He needed to get on his feet, get to water, and then find shelter so he could assess his wounds. He pushed again, but the pain that swept over him made Adam realize he would not be walking anywhere. His leg was either broken or badly sprained.

He lay down again and panted for a while. The world seemed to disappear as he fought the waves of pain. Anguish that was as much mental as physical racked him. Adam didn't want to die. He would not die.

He got up on his elbows again and dragged his body forward, bracing against the pain caused by moving his injured leg. Slanted ground helped him reach the stream. He ducked his head in the cold, clear water for a moment and came up spluttering. He used his right hand as a scoop and drank deeply. Renewed strength flowed through him with the water.

After slaking the worst of his thirst, Adam grabbed the trunk of a young poplar and pulled himself into a seated position to take stock. His leg was causing the worst of his pain, but his arms and face had been scratched and scraped as he fell down the ravine. He was lucky that his wounds were so minor.

Minor! He laughed at the word. He was in a tight fix, and

he knew it. The chance that he would survive seemed very small, but as long as he had strength, he had to try.

He turned his head at the sound of crunching leaves. His attackers? A bear? His heartbeat tripled its thumps in his chest.

Then he saw what was making the noise. A rabbit hopped its way across fallen limbs and approached the stream a few feet away. What Adam wouldn't give for his rifle. That fat rabbit looked like a mighty fine meal.

The rabbit must have sensed the danger because it reversed course and disappeared back into the woods.

His gaze followed the path of the animal, and then he saw it. A cabin! Shelter! It was only a few yards away from his position, but he'd been so focused on reaching the stream he'd not even seen it.

"Hello the house." His voice rasped the greeting that would reassure the owner he was not an Indian brave. No one responded, but because his hoarse call might not have been heard, he tried again. "Hello the house!" This time his voice was stronger. Adam waited for any inhabitant to respond, but only the noise of the forest answered him.

Maybe whoever lived there was out setting or checking traps. This far away from the safety of a settlement, the cabin was likely occupied by a trapper. Adam hoped he would at least help him with his leg and feed him so he'd have a chance to get back to civilization.

Whatever the outcome, he knew he could not remain in the open. But before he began dragging himself to the door of the cabin, he would need something to support his leg. A good bit of deadfall lay within reach. He chose a limb that was as big around as his arm. He pulled off his grimy overcoat and turned it inside out, stopping to rest for a few moments after the effort.

Adam reached for his hunting knife, thankful to feel its reassuring hilt under his fingers. With a satisfied grunt, he went to work cutting out the coat's lining and tearing it into strips. He laid the limb against his leg and bound it with the strips from his coat. Another large limb would serve as a crutch to help him keep his weight off his injured leg.

Using the sapling and the second limb, Adam pulled himself up. The world around him lost some definition, but he managed to get to his feet. With a stilted, shuffling movement, he lurched forward. One step. Rest. Another step. Rest. Thirty-two steps and rests got him to the door of the cabin.

What he saw carved into the rough planks made him groan in despair. Three letters—GTT. Gone to Texas. The cabin was abandoned. He would find no help here.

Adam looked up at the sky. *What now, God? Are You through with me yet? Or do You have other plans in mind?*

God didn't answer, of course. Proving again that He did not exist. Or if He did, He had no concern for mortals.

Adam forced the door open and made his slow way into the cabin. It was a single room with sparse furnishings: a square table, one chair, and a straw sleeping mat. But it represented shelter. He held on to the wall and made his way to the fireplace. It was cold, of course, but a sizable log still lay in it; a few smaller logs were stacked to one side.

Adam spied a chunk of flint on the rough mantelpiece and knew he would soon have warmth. He steeled himself to ignore the pain in his leg as he worked to ensure his survival. A few of the cotton strips from his coat lining made a combustible ball which he placed on the sooty back log. He broke smaller twigs off the firewood and tented them above the cotton. Striking his knife against the flint created molten chips that soon ignited the cotton and twigs. With a satisfied grunt, he added a couple of logs and soon had a blaze going.

A rumbling sound filled the small room. Food was his next problem, as his stomach had reminded him. He forced himself up once more and continued his exploration. Two wooden barrels in one corner revealed dried corn and sprouted potatoes. His stomach rumbled again, and his mouth watered. He picked up a potato. It was soft but still edible.

He also discovered a pair of identical clay jugs. He picked one up, surprised to find it so heavy. He uncorked it and sniffed the contents. Moonshine. A satisfied sound escaped him. The alcohol would come in handy to cleanse his wounds.

The voice of his stern father echoed in Adam's head. *Alcohol is the devil's brew. It makes fools of wise men and drowns the morals of saints.* Well, no need to worry about that. He would only use it to cleanse his wounds. . .and perhaps take a swallow or two to dull the pain in his leg.

three

Iris tucked a curl under the brim of her riding cap and encouraged her horse, Button, along the road. Brooding white clouds seemed to press down on her shoulders, spewing out fat, lazy flakes that clung to her mittens or melted into her horse's mane.

She pushed Button to a canter. This morning when she'd volunteered to take supplies to Grandpa and Grandma Taylor, her ma had been doubtful. But Iris had been sure she could make the trip before the roads became treacherous. She shook her head. It was far too late to turn back now.

At least she wasn't cooped up at home this afternoon. The thought replaced her concern with the exhilaration of freedom. She loved her family, but spending all of her waking hours in close quarters with them had made her as fidgety as a squirrel. It would be fun to sit by the fire and listen to her grandparents talk about the days when Ma was a little girl. And Grandma probably had something really good to eat, too.

She cantered around a curve and saw her grandparents' house tucked next to their large barn. A relieved sigh escaped her frozen lips. "Whoa, Button." Iris pulled on the reins as she reached the front yard. A curl of smoke rose from the chimney, drifting upward to mingle with the low-lying clouds. She dismounted and pulled off the heavy saddlebags her parents had packed with a ham, a roast, and some of the sugared peach chips her grandma loved.

Grandpa Taylor stomped out onto the front porch, a wool scarf tucked around his ears. His bald head gleamed in the muted light, its smooth surface reminding her of a hen's egg. He followed her to the barn and dragged the door open, pointing her toward an empty stall. "Is everything okay at home?"

Iris nodded as she unsaddled her horse and rubbed him down. "I had to get out of there, though. Eli has a cold, and Ma is making her special liniment to rub on his chest." She wrinkled her nose. "I know it'll make him feel better, but it sure makes the house smell awful."

Grandpa waited for her to exit the stall before fastening the door. "It's a wonder you made it in this weather, but I'm glad you're here." He raised an eyebrow at her. "You'll never guess who has come over to visit today. Wohali and Noya."

"Aunt Noya and Uncle Wohali!" Iris named the Cherokee couple who had been her grandparents' neighbors since before she was born. She grabbed her mittens and followed her grandpa back to the house, thinking of the days when she was younger. She had often played over at their house while Ma and Grandma pieced together quilts. They had a grandniece, Kamama, who was about Iris's age and who had visited them often. Maybe she could find out what Kamama was doing now that they were all grown-up.

Iris stamped the snow and mud off her boots before entering her grandparents' home.

Warm air and the scent of cinnamon welcomed her. Grandma and Aunt Noya were sitting in rocking chairs in front of the fireplace, while Uncle Wohali sat nearby in a straight chair, whittling at a small piece of wood. Grandma was rolling yarn into a ball while Aunt Noya held the newly spun wool in her hand to prevent tangling. They were laughing exuberantly as Iris and her grandfather entered.

Grandma leaned her head back as she laughed. Her hair had been knotted into a loose bun, and she wore a lacy shawl around her shoulders to combat any stray drafts.

Aunt Noya's dark hair had developed a few streaks of gray and reflected the light of the fire she sat in front of.

"What are you two laughing about?" asked Grandpa.

Grandma looked up, dropped her ball of yarn, and clapped her hands together. "It's so good to see you, Iris." She pushed herself up slowly and reached for the black walnut cane Grandpa had made for her last year.

Aunt Noya stood and waited until Iris and her grandma had shared a brief hug before stepping forward. "*Osiyo*, my friend." She used the Cherokee word for hello, her deep voice filled with warmth and welcome.

"Osiyo." Iris threw her arms around the older lady.

She turned to Uncle Wohali, who was awaiting his turn. "Osiyo."

Grandpa grabbed another chair from its peg on the wall and placed it close to the fireplace. "What's the news from your house?"

Even though Grandma and Grandpa had already heard about the Christmas Eve party, Iris gave them a humorous accounting for Uncle Wohali and Aunt Noya's benefit. The quizzical looks on their faces as she described apple bobbing made Iris laugh. No matter that they had lived among white people for two decades or more, some of the traditions still seemed odd to the Indian couple.

"And what happens to the apples that were missed?" Aunt Noya wanted to know.

Iris had to admit she'd never considered the question, but she guessed they went into apple pies or sauce. Whatever the purpose, they would not have gone to waste. Fresh fruit was far too precious, even in a city that bustled with traders.

Grandma finished rolling her yarn and drew out a pair of needles to begin knitting.

"What are you making, Grandma?"

Her grandmother glanced up and smiled. "A new pair of socks for your grandpa. The last time I did the mending, I noticed he had several pairs with more holes than threads."

Grandpa looked a bit sheepish, but he did not contradict her.

Aunt Noya walked to the kitchen area and began collecting dishes with easy familiarity. "Get the blackberry pie and bring it to the table, Iris."

She spotted the lidded iron pot perched on the far edge of the large fireplace. Her mouth began to water. She loved Grandma's fruit pies made in a dutch oven. They always had such flaky crusts and intense fruity flavor. "Blackberry pie is my favorite."

Grandpa removed the coffeepot from its hook on the fireplace while Uncle Wohali tucked his whittling back in his pocket and put his knife in its beaded holster. The reserved Indian stood and picked up an armful of logs, tossing them on the fire to keep it from dying. They all seemed to have their appointed tasks, and they worked together without speaking.

Iris helped move their chairs around the dining table and made sure that a pitcher of fresh cream was placed in the center of the table.

Grandma didn't move from her rocker until everyone else sat down. Then she put away her chain of stitches and joined them at the table. According to established custom, they all linked hands while Grandpa blessed the food.

Iris was so glad she'd made the trip this afternoon. A relaxing visit was exactly what she had needed to combat the fidgets that had been plaguing her for the last few days.

She poured some milk into her cup of steaming coffee and added a dollop of cream to her dish of pie. "How is Kamama doing?"

A gentle smile crossed Aunt Noya's face. "Our niece has gone back to the village where she was raised to take the message of salvation to her family."

Iris forgot all about the food on the table. "How wonderful! The last time I saw her, Kamama was more worried about clothing styles than witnessing. What changed her mind?"

Uncle Wohali, a man Iris could never have accused of being talkative, spoke up. "Her cousin was killed in a fight several months ago. He was not a Christian." His face was as hard as granite.

Iris thought of how she would feel in his place. "How awful. I know that must have hurt all of you."

Aunt Noya reached a hand to her husband. "To know that you will never again see a loved one in this life or the next is a very difficult thing."

Grandpa cleared his throat and leaned forward. "It's very courageous of Kamama to use the tragedy for good. Before she left, she told Martha and me that her desire is to make sure no other Cherokee has to die without hearing the teaching of Christ."

"Yes," Grandma agreed, a smile of sympathy deepening the soft wrinkles on her face. "I know you miss her greatly."

Iris looked at the people around the table as they talked of the Indians who still had not heard of Christ's message. She almost envied Kamama for her sense of purpose. She would much rather it had not taken such a tragedy, but at least some good would come from the untimely death of Kamama's cousin.

She thought of Paul's promise in Romans that *"all things work together for good to them that love God."* When she was younger, she'd thought the verse meant that only good things would happen to the people who loved God, but now she thought that Paul was trying to encourage early Christians by explaining that all things—the good events as well as the bad ones—were tools God used to bring blessings to His people.

She reached into the pocket of her skirt and pulled out the familiar newsprint advertisement. How many times had she unfolded it and read it? How many nights had she clutched it in her hands as she prayed for guidance. Iris dreamed of making her life count for something more than attending parties and bobbing for apples. Would she be able to find God's path for her life like Kamama had done? Or would she waste away here, an object of pity to her neighbors? When would her time come? Or would it? Would her family shield her from danger so assiduously that she never had the chance to fulfill her dreams?

⁂

Iris bent over the buckskin breeches her young brother had torn, punching her needle through the thick hide. "I wish Eli would be more careful with his clothing."

Ma stirred a large pot of stew that smelled wonderful. "He's too busy to be careful, dear. A lot of work didn't get done while he was laid up in bed with that terrible fever last week."

"I was worried he would never stop coughing, but that nasty-smelling salve really eased his congestion."

"Thank the Lord." Ma bowed her head, and Iris knew she was repeating her thanks to God. After a moment she looked up and smiled widely. "I'm so thankful the rest of us avoided catching it. I can remember past winters when it seemed that you and your sister and brother passed sickness back and forth for weeks on end."

"That must have been hard for you, Ma. How did you cope with all three of us being sick at the same time?"

Ma moved to the table and diced a few more potatoes. "Although I spent a great deal of time worrying about you and praying for your recovery, the actual work wasn't difficult.

When you have your own children, you'll understand." She added the potatoes to the stewpot and began stirring once more. "Now that Eli's fully recovered, his appetite is back. Whether he's careful with those breeches or not, he'll soon outgrow them."

"That's true," Iris agreed. She set a final stitch, tied a knot in the thread, and cut it with a satisfied smile. She held the breeches up to inspect her work. "Should I also let out the waist?"

Ma shook her head. "Those ought to have enough room for now. But I'm sure your brother will need them loosened in a month or so."

Iris leaned back in her chair and breathed in the pleasant aroma of the bubbling stew. "Is Pa going to bring us some sassafras root to boil? I've been wanting some for weeks now. Ever since Aunt Dolly's Christmas dinner, as a matter of fact. She always has the best tasting sassafras tea."

The sound of hoofbeats stopped their conversation. Ma put the lid on her pot and turned to the door. "Speaking of your pa, I imagine that's him now. He went into town early this morning."

Iris would have asked why, but the door swung open as her pa walked into the house.

"How are the most beautiful women in Davidson County doing this fine morning?" He caught his wife in a hug and placed a loud kiss on her cheek. Then he turned to Iris and grabbed her from her chair, swinging her around like she weighed only a few pounds. "I have news that both of you are going to want to hear."

When Pa placed her back on her feet, Iris put her hands on her hips and looked at him. "What is it, Pa?"

"Yes, tell us your news, Asher."

Iris wished she could stop time and savor this moment.

Her ma practically glowed with love now that Pa was home. And Pa, dressed in a black suit, white shirt, and black cravat, was the very picture of the gentleman farmer. Iris wondered if he ever regretted giving up his financial career to work the soil. Of course his political aspirations had ended before he and Ma even married. Still, by the accounts of her aunt and grandparents, her pa had been poised to become one of Andrew Jackson's most trusted advisers. But he'd turned down the opportunity to travel the world with the famous and popular president.

Her pa reached into his coat and produced several folded sheets of ivory paper with a flourish. "Guess who has sent us a letter?"

Iris mentioned Pa's younger sister. "Aunt Mary?"

Ma clasped her hands and rested them against her chin. "My sister, Eleanor?"

Pa shook his head at both of them.

"Has Uncle Donny written from Philadelphia?"

"Nope. That's three guesses. Do you give up?"

At their nods he lowered the stationery so they could see the return address printed above the wax seal.

"Pastor Miller?" Ma's voice was a squeal of joy.

"Yes." Pa winked at Iris. "And there's even a separate note inside from Camie."

"Camie wrote to me?" Iris's heart leaped. She grabbed for the letter but was frustrated as her pa lifted it up over his head.

Hannah, Iris's younger sister, ran in as they were trying to grab the sheets. "Whatever are you doing?" She took the chair her sister had recently vacated and clambered atop it. With her additional height, it was easy for her to reach Pa's hand. She grabbed the letter with a triumphant squeak.

Iris was not about to tolerate her younger sister stealing the letter. "Give it to me. You don't even remember Camie."

"I do, too." Hannah stuck out her tongue at Iris. "She's that blond girl who used to come over and help us shell peas."

"That's enough, you two." Ma interrupted them before a fight could break out. "Give me the letter, Hannah. I'll read it out loud so we can all enjoy it at the same time."

Iris was chastened by her mother's admonition. "I'll do better, Ma. I promise."

She silently berated herself while her parents talked about the family who used to live in Nashville. Besides being Aunt Dolly's pastor, Reverend Miller, along with his wife, had built and managed a school for the local Indians. Iris and her family had worked at the school as she grew up, infusing her with the desire to do something important with her life. The Millers' daughter, Camie, had been one of her best friends. They had even been baptized together on a cool Sunday morning in the calm blue waters of a small stream just outside the city.

Iris had cried for days when Reverend Miller announced that he had been called to work at Brainerd Mission near an Indian settlement on the Tennessee River called Ross's Landing. She and Camie had hugged and made promises to always stay in touch. But it was hard to fulfill that promise. The years went by. Camie had married a fine Christian man, a surveyor who had come to work in the area and decided to stay after falling in love with her. Iris wished she could have gone to the wedding, but her parents had been unable to leave at that time and unwilling to send her alone. It was the story of her life. They didn't want to let her out of their sight.

Pa cleared his throat and put a hand on her ma's arm before she could start reading the letter she held. "I read the letter before coming home, and Reverend Miller mentioned something we need to discuss."

Ma folded the stationery. "What is it, Asher?"

He gazed at his hands for a moment before speaking. Iris wondered what could be wrong. She held her breath and concentrated her attention on him.

"Reverend Miller mentioned in his letter that Camie has decided to give up her job as nanny to take care of her own children."

Ma's brow wrinkled. "Wasn't she caring for some Cherokee orphans?"

"That's right. Their parents died, and they are living with their grandfather. Camie was hired not only to care for the children but also to teach them how to live in a white man's world. A house slave has been looking after them ever since Camie left several months before her babies were born. The little girls' grandfather has not been able to find a suitable replacement yet." Pa glanced toward Iris. "Reverend Miller is hoping we can suggest someone to take her place. It would have to be a young Christian lady of excellent reputation."

At first his words did not penetrate fully. Then their import seemed to explode in her mind. "Me! I can go and take Camie's place."

Her parents exchanged a long look. Iris could feel the excitement bursting out like sunshine after a week of rain. "Please, Pa. You have to say yes. You know it's right."

"I don't know, Iris." Ma's voice sounded troubled. "Your pa and I will talk about it."

"But Ma! It'll be perfect. I will be right there in the same town with Camie and her family. They live so close to Reverend and Mrs. Miller. You know they'll watch over me as closely as you and Pa do. I have to do this."

"Iris, I knew what your reaction would be from the moment I read Reverend Miller's correspondence." Pa walked to where her ma still sat with the letter in her lap. "I've been praying about what to say since I left Nashville."

Iris could feel her heart thumping in her chest. They had to let her go. It was too perfect. She pulled the dog-eared advertisement from the pocket of her skirt. "I've been reading this article nearly every day for the past three months and praying God would either find a way to send me to teach or take the desire from my heart." She paused for a breath. "The desire is still there, and I truly believe He is showing me the way."

"Although that part of Tennessee is not as settled as we are here, you wouldn't be going to some frontier town in the wilds of Texas," her ma cautioned. "And being a nanny to two young girls is not the same as a teaching position. It will only be a temporary situation at best."

Iris shook her head. "I know that, but once I am out there, God may open the way to other jobs. If not, I could always come back to Nashville. When I found out that Kamama had gone to witness to the people in her village, I began to understand that there are many opportunities to serve God by serving others. I even thought maybe one of my aunts or uncles would need to have me come in the same way that you moved to town to take care of Aunt Dolly, Ma. But no one needed me, so I went back to the advertisement in the newspaper. I thought maybe everything would work out so I could go there. But I always knew it was a remote possibility."

Ma held out a hand to Pa. "I have to admit it causes me much less worry to think of your going to be in the same area as the Millers, but there are other matters we should consider. I rely on your help here, Iris."

Hannah had been so quiet during the discussion that Iris had nearly forgotten her sister was in the room until she spoke. "I can take over Iris's chores, Ma."

Iris beamed at her younger sister. She had never expected

Hannah to come to her assistance. "See, Ma? We can work it out."

"I don't know." Ma turned to Pa. "What do you think?"

Iris could see the answer in his eyes. He thought it was a good idea. They were going to let her go! She would get to see another part of Tennessee and live close to her best friend! Iris wanted to jump up and down. But this was not the time to make either of her parents question her maturity. She would have to maintain her dignity until she could get off by herself.

"Maybe Hannah and I should go out to the springhouse and get some fresh milk while you and Pa discuss it."

"Don't you want to read your note?" Ma asked.

Iris nodded. She broke the seal with one tip of her finger, careful to avoid destruction of the stationery. From now on she would be on her guard at all times and show her parents just how self-controlled their elder daughter could be.

At least while anyone was around to see her.

four

Daisy, Tennessee
February 1836

The stagecoach driver jerked the door open, startling the passengers from various stages of slumber. "We're at Poe's Crossroads, young lady."

A blush crept into Iris's cheeks as she tried to understand why the coachman was beckoning toward her. "But I'm supposed to be going to Daisy, Tennessee."

The driver rolled his eyes, showing his disgust for her ignorance. "They're one and the same. Daisy's the name of the town, but this is the crossroads where the stage stops. Did you expect me to take you to your doorstep?"

Reassured, Iris inched forward, trying not to jostle the sleeping child on her right. Mr. Howington, the middle-aged gentleman sitting in the position opposite hers, offered her a hand. She had been miffed at Pa for treating her like a baby by asking Mr. Howington to watch over her during the overland trip from Nashville, but she had to admit that he'd made the journey much more bearable. When they'd stopped for meals, he'd been her escort. Each evening when they reached a coaching inn, he'd made sure that some other female—whether the innkeeper's daughter or a female passenger—slept in the same room with her so that her reputation would be protected. If not for his persistence, on several occasions she would not have received fresh water to wash away the day's dusty travel. He'd even shared his food with her on those days that the coachman had decided to press on rather than stop for a midday meal. But perhaps most importantly, Mr. Howington had always made sure she occupied the seat directly behind the driver. The other passengers had grumbled a bit since that position inside the coach endured the least number of bumps and jars, but they had backed down in the face of his firm insistence.

"Thank you so much, Mr. Howington." Iris allowed him to pull her forward until she could stand up, albeit with a rather hunched stance. "I can never repay your kindness."

"That's quite all right, Miss Landon. I would only hope some other gentleman might do the same favor for any daughter of mine."

In the crowded interior of the coach, Iris did not have enough room to give the dear man a hug so she contented herself with squeezing his hand. "Godspeed."

One of the other passengers yawned while a grouchy man frowned at her. "Would you go on and get out so we can get on our way? I've got to get to Washington before Friday."

Another blush suffused Iris's cheeks. She had overheard the bad-tempered man offering a bonus to the stagecoach driver to get him to his destination early. Not only had that meant long days on the coach, it also meant she had a problem. Camie and her husband would not expect her to arrive tonight. As she inched her way past the feet, bags, and boxes of the passengers, Iris wondered how she would arrange transportation to their home.

She stepped to the ground with a sigh of relief and took a moment to thank God for her safe arrival. A thump to her right made Iris jump back and stumble against the outside of the coach. Her trunk lay in the dusty road at her feet. A grunt warned her just in time. Iris looked up to see her portmanteau, the large case that held her dearest possessions, sail through the air to land neatly atop the trunk. She winced, hoping the bottle of expensive French perfume from Grandma Landon had survived the coachman's callous treatment.

Iris would have complained about his roughness with her items, but the coachman had already regained his bench on the front of the large coach. He whipped up the team of four horses without a backward glance, and the equipage careened around a corner and disappeared.

"Well, I never." Iris looked around her at the tiny town that was to be her new home. What she could see in the gloom of late evening was not inspiring. Only three or four buildings seemed to make up the town of Daisy, and only one of those was lit up. There were no lights outside, of course. Not that she'd expected them. This was not Nashville, after all. It was barely a community. According to the description Camie had sent, only a few dozen families lived on this side of the Tennessee River, although more settlers were beginning to make their way here. The other side of the river was mostly Indian Territory, although it did boast a trading post, called Ross's Landing, and Brainerd Mission, where Reverend and Mrs. Miller lived.

Iris wondered if she could walk to Camie's house but realized she didn't even know which way to go. Tears burned at the corners of her eyes. Whenever she'd imagined arriving, it had been in the middle of the day, not during the gloom of night and not a whole day ahead of schedule. What was she supposed to do?

The cool night air nipped at her cheeks as she wondered if the town of Daisy boasted an inn. She drew her shoulders back in an effort to bolster her waning confidence and walked down the street in search of a likely prospect.

Raucous laughter spewed from the one lit building in town.

It must be a tavern. Iris took a step in that direction. Perhaps they could direct her to the Sherers' home or at least rent her a room for the evening. Another roar of laughter slowed her. She tilted her head and listened intently. Someone played a piano, and a lady sang. It sounded like a friendly place. She pasted a smile on her face, gripped her reticule tightly, and stepped past the hitching post onto the raised walkway that ran the length of the building.

As Iris reached out a tentative hand toward the door, it swung outward. A man exited precipitously, barreling into her and pushing her down. Her teeth clacked together. "Well, I never!"

"What are you doing on t' ground?" His slurred voice indicated that the man had been imbibing. "Here." He leaned over and offered his hand.

Iris wanted to burst into tears. Maybe she was having a bad dream. But then why did the ground under her feel so solid? She put her hand in the stranger's and allowed him to help her up. Her nose wrinkled at the smell of whiskey. In their work with the Indians at home, her parents had often had to deal with Indians who had imbibed too much "firewater."

The stranger bowed, still holding onto her hand. "Adam Stuart's m' name."

Iris didn't know how to answer him. She should have been embarrassed by his casual manners. Back home she would never have considered speaking to a man without a proper introduction. And she certainly wouldn't allow him to continue holding her hand. She gave a tug and pulled free.

He pointed a finger at her. "Why are you wandering outside all alone?"

Some part of her mind noticed that Mr. Stuart was tall, taller than she. He had a square chin and even features—she might even call him handsome if he was sober. His eyes were large and appeared brown in the muted light. They shone with intelligence and something else—was it vulnerability? Pain? For a brief instant, she wanted to comfort him.

What was she thinking? Offer comfort to a complete stranger? Iris shook her head and immediately put a hand up to keep her hat from falling off. Her pins must have loosened while she napped in the coach, and then her jarring tumble had made the situation more tenuous. Now her hair seemed determined to escape captivity. She fought the heavy curls, tucking them away with little success. Finally she gave up to concentrate on her main problem. "I need to find Lance and Camie Sherer."

Mr. Stuart turned in a circle. "I don't see them."

"Of course not." Iris wanted to scream her frustration. Why did Mr. Stuart have to be drunk? "They are probably at home. I need someone to help me get to the home of Mr. Lance Sherer."

He frowned and stroked his chin with a finger as if deep in thought.

Iris waited a moment or two for him to answer. She had opened her mouth to ask him again when he dropped his hand and nodded at her.

"Lance Sherer. Nice man. Very smart. He already has a wife, y'know. And children." He hiccuped and smiled at her. A dimple appeared in his left cheek, making him appear debonair in spite of the wrinkled condition of his dark suit.

"Well, I never!" Her indignation made her splutter the words. What was the man thinking? "I am a good friend of his wife. I've come at her suggestion."

"Is there a problem here?" Unnoticed, another man had stepped through the doors of the tavern.

Foreboding made Iris's heart thump loudly. Now she faced two strangers, and both of them were likely inebriated. What should she do? Cry for help? Make a dash through the door of the tavern? Or would that land her in even more trouble?

She took a deep breath to calm her fears and glanced at the second stranger. At least he seemed to be able to stand straight without aid. And he was tall, too. Were all the men tall in this part of Tennessee? She couldn't believe that her first two encounters in Daisy were with men she had to look up to.

In appearance the second stranger was the opposite of the amiable man behind her. His hair was blond, and his shoulders were straight and wide. She couldn't tell for certain in the dim light, but Iris thought his eyes were either blue or green. His style of dress was different, too—buckskin pants and a fur-lined coat instead of a crumpled suit. He carried a wide-brimmed hat in one hand, which he swept in an arc as he bowed to her. "Nathan Pierce at your service, miss."

Iris didn't know whether she should laugh or cry. Here she was stuck in the middle of nowhere, all her worldly goods lying in the street, and presented with two different men— one a charming rogue and the other a model of propriety. Except. . . If Mr. Nathan Pierce was such an upright citizen, what was he doing coming out of the tavern?

Another wave of laughter from inside suggested that the three of them would soon be joined by other examples of the male population to be found in Daisy.

"Do you know where Mr. and Mrs. Lance Sherer live?"

Mr. Pierce inclined his head over his right shoulder. "About two miles down that road."

Two more men stumbled out of the tavern. One of them stared at her but moved past without saying anything when he caught the warning look in Mr. Pierce's eyes.

Mr. Pierce returned his gaze to her face. "I can take you there, if you'd like."

Iris wondered if the stranger was trustworthy. But what

other option did she have? She couldn't stay out here in the street all night.

"Don't pay att. . .att'ntion to him." Mr. Stuart's words were still as slurred as when he'd first come outside, even though the crisp night air should have penetrated the fog of alcohol. He grabbed hold of the hitching post and leaned against it. "I c'n take care of you."

Mr. Pierce deftly inserted himself between them. He held out his arm. "Ignore him. Mr. Stuart is too. . .tired. . .to recall his manners."

Iris certainly couldn't fault Mr. Pierce's manners. Mr. Stuart was obviously not tired. But she appreciated Mr. Pierce's kindness in trying to shield her from the man's boorishness. Maybe it would be safe to allow him to take her to the Sherers' home. She was about to tell him so when she remembered her trunk and portmanteau. She glanced around him to the street. From the corner of her vision she saw Mr. Stuart make a shaky bow and stagger away. She returned her attention to Mr. Pierce.

"Don't worry about your things. I'll have someone come back in the wagon and pick them up. When you wake up in the morning, everything will be there."

"I cannot thank you enough, Mr. Pierce." She put her hand on his arm, impressed by how hard his muscles felt under the thick fur coat.

"It's my pleasure, Miss. . . ?"

"Landon."

"Miss Landon." He led her to a tall roan stallion. "May I?"

Iris nodded and found herself picked up and tossed into the Spanish-style saddle. It was a good thing she'd spent time riding bareback, or she might have fallen since there was no place to hook her knee without immodestly displaying her ankles. Mr. Pierce mounted behind her and put an arm around her waist. Now she was safe from falling, but what about her reputation?

With a tiny shrug, she decided there was little choice if she wished to reach Camie's home tonight. And what was the alternative? Taking her chances with the charming drunk? Not a good idea. She relaxed as she realized that Mr. Pierce was not going to take advantage of the situation.

"How do you know the Sherers?" His deep voice tickled her ear.

"Camie's father, Reverend Miller, built a school for the Indians around the Nashville area, and my parents were very involved in its mission to teach English and spread the message of salvation. Camie and I worked and played together there. We were as close as sisters growing up."

"I see."

Silence grew between them, punctuated by the steady hoofbeats of his horse. Iris tried to force her tired mind to come up with another topic of conversation. "Have you seen her little girls?"

"No." He shifted in the saddle. "Children make me nervous."

"That's because they're not yours."

Whatever his answer would have been was lost as they turned off the road toward a house that stood some feet away. It huddled at the edge of a dense forest, every window dark and shuttered against the night.

"They are not expecting you?" Mr. Pierce asked.

"Not exactly." The Sherers were to meet her. But she had never imagined that her arrival would be twelve hours early.

"Hello the house!" Mr. Pierce's yell ended her introspection. She waited while he dismounted and reached up to lift her down, once again marveling at the fact that he was so tall. Once her feet were on the ground, Iris actually had to bend her head back to meet his gaze.

Mr. Pierce escorted Iris to the front door with the same easy confidence he'd shown since they met. She deeply appreciated his taking charge because she felt overwhelmed. She stood to one side as he banged on the door. At first no sound came from inside the Sherer house, but then she heard heavy footfalls on the staircase. Yellow light flickered around the outer edge of the front door as it opened.

"Nathan Pierce? What brings you out in the middle of the night?" Lance Sherer's voice was deep and authoritative.

"I'm sorry for disturbing you, Lance." Her escort was nothing if not polite. Iris admired politeness. Her parents had stressed the finer points of social niceties, saying that living in the country was no excuse for poor manners. Apparently Mr. Pierce's parents agreed with that philosophy. "I have brought a friend of your family." He glanced back to where she stood. "Miss Landon was recently delivered to us by stage."

"Iris?" Camie's husband stepped onto the narrow porch, a candle in one hand and a rifle tucked under his other elbow. "Is it really you?" He leaned the rifle against the doorjamb and beckoned to them to enter.

She nodded and stepped forward with a little hiccup of relief mixed with tiredness. "It's so good to meet you."

Mr. Sherer was not as tall as the other two men she'd met tonight, destroying Iris's earlier hope that all the men in this part of Tennessee would make her feel of normal height. Strands of dark brown hair straggled across his forehead, but her attention was caught by his wide blue eyes. They were so kind and calm, so full of welcome. She liked him immediately and could see why Camie had fallen in love with him. Everything about him, from his warm smile to his beckoning hand gestures, made her feel welcome.

"Camie, it's your friend Iris." He looked over his shoulder to address his wife, who must have been standing on the stairway. "She's come to us early." Camie's husband turned back to look past her. "Where are your bags?"

"They're back in town, lying in the middle of the road." Iris forced the words between stiff lips. Irritation straightened her spine as she remembered the callous coachman.

Mr. Pierce diverted her thoughts by gently taking her hand and pressing a warm kiss on her gloved fingers. "I hope to see you again soon."

He was such a nice man. "I hope so, too." Iris couldn't help being flattered by the obvious admiration in his voice. She watched him stride back to his horse before stepping back to allow Mr. Sherer to close the door.

She forgot all about Mr. Pierce as she suddenly found herself wrapped in Camie's tight hug. Her irritation and exhaustion disappeared as her tears mixed with those of her friend.

Camie was all grown up. Gone was the shy girl she remembered—in her place was a beautiful young matron. She was dressed in a flannel gown of pale blue that flattered her delicate complexion. Her honey gold hair was plaited and hung down her back like a silk rope. She had thrown a cotton wrap over her shoulders before coming downstairs, and she hugged it to her as protection against the cold night air.

Camie picked up a candle that was sitting on the table next to the front door and lit it from her husband's before handing it to Iris. With the additional light, Iris could make out the wide foyer with doors off to the right and left. She guessed that one led to the parlor and the other perhaps to a dining room or the kitchen.

Mr. Sherer looked at Camie. "I wonder if I should saddle a horse and go help him with Miss Landon's bags."

"Please don't stand on ceremony, Mr. Sherer. I hope you will call me Iris."

His nod seemed to hold approval. "I would be delighted, if you'll return the favor and call me Lance."

"I doubt you should make the effort to go back into town, dear." Camie raised an eyebrow in an expression of mischief that took Iris back to their shared childhood. "It would take you too long to saddle the horse. Besides, you need to give Mr. Pierce the chance to impress our Iris with his chivalry."

Iris looked down at her gloved hands, surprised that the candlelight showed how much dirt had accumulated on the white material. She wanted nothing more than to wash up, fall in bed, and sleep for two or three days.

"Tell me all about your trip." Camie pulled her plaited hair over her shoulder. "Was it scary? Did you have any trouble on the way? Why did you get here in the middle of the night?"

"Now Camie." Her husband shook his head. "There will be plenty of time for you to catch up on the news tomorrow. Why don't you get Iris upstairs to a bedchamber? I'm sure she's about to drop where she stands."

Camie sighed but nodded. "You're right, of course." She lit another candle and led the way upstairs. "I can't wait to hear all about your journey."

"And I can't wait to see your daughters." The hallway at the top of the stairs disappeared into shadowy darkness their candles barely penetrated. Iris followed Camie past two doorways to a third that was closed.

"They are adorable. Like the dolls we played with when we were little girls."

"Only better." Iris noticed a framed sampler hanging on the wall, but it was too dark for her to see its details.

"They have taught me so much." Camie's serious voice drew Iris's attention away from the wall. "I understand the love of God like I never did before." She opened the third door. "Here we are."

Iris wanted to ask about her comment, but it was late. She watched as Camie bustled over to the bed and patted the mattress. "I can ask Lance to bring up some coals so you can have a fire while you undress."

"Don't worry about that." Iris could almost feel the softness of the sheets enveloping her. "But I do need a nightgown since my bags are still in town."

"Of course." Camie clucked her tongue against the roof of her mouth. "What kind of hostess must you think I am?"

Iris put her candle on a tall dressing table that was angled in a corner to one side of the fireplace. "How could you know that I would arrive with only the clothes I am standing in?"

As Camie disappeared into the dark hallway, Iris could hear her still bemoaning the failure to anticipate her guest's needs.

While she waited, Iris pulled off her hat and let her hair cascade down with a sense of relief. She could hear pins plinking on the wooden floor where it was not protected by Camie's rug. She pulled off her gloves and placed them next to her candle. The air in the bedroom was quite nippy, but she had no doubt that she would warm up quickly once she buried herself under those inviting quilts.

While she waited for her friend to return, Iris rinsed her face and hands with water from a washbowl. It was a relief to rid herself of some of the grit from her travels even though the cold water stole her breath away for a moment.

"Here we go." Camie reentered with a thick cotton nightdress over her arm. "Oh my! I had forgotten how curly your hair is. Would you like me to plait it for you?"

Iris shook her head, sending the brown tendrils flying in several directions. "I have lots of practice. Go on back to bed. You need your sleep. I'll be fine." To prove her point, she scraped her hair back with nimble fingers and twisted it into submission.

"Well, if you need anything else, just call out. We're right down the hall." Camie laid the nightdress across her bed and left her.

It wasn't long before Iris was in bed, the weight of the heavy quilts pushing her into the softness of the mattress. After thanking God for bringing her safely to her destination and asking for His protection over her loved ones, Iris let her thoughts drift to Camie's statement about her little girls. Did God take the same pleasure in the birth of each of His children? What a wonderful thought.

She burrowed down into the bed, her mind filled with praise for the loving God who provided a way for showing her how wide and deep His love ran.

❧

An insistent tapping sound roused Iris. For a moment she didn't recognize her surroundings, but then she remembered. Her life was really beginning. She had made it to Daisy and to the Sherers' home. The sound was someone knocking at her door. "Come in."

"Well, Sleeping Beauty." Camie entered the room with a large wooden tray balanced in her hands. She had pulled her hair back and twisted it into a bun. Several strands had worked free already and framed her face. Her gray dress was accented with a darker gray collar and cuffs, and a starched white apron protected her skirt. She was the very picture of a matron. "I finally decided I'd have to come up here and rouse you if I was ever going to find out about all the people back in Nashville. I hope you still have a prodigious memory."

Iris sniffed the air appreciatively. "Is that breakfast?"

With a nod, Camie placed the tray on the edge of the bed. Iris could see a stack of fluffy batter cakes, fried eggs, a small mountain of bacon strips, potatoes, and biscuits. "I'm hungry, but I couldn't eat half of all the food you brought up here."

"I'm going to help, silly." Camie divided the food between two plates and handed one to Iris. "Lance is watching the girls while you and I eat breakfast. They woke up around daybreak, but since you were sleeping so peacefully, I took them downstairs."

"It's so good to be here." Iris dug into her breakfast with gusto.

"What was your trip like?"

"Crowded and dusty. I don't know why they have to put so many people in one coach. There was always an elbow in my side and some stranger's knee pressed against my leg." She rolled her eyes. "And the driver was the surliest man you can imagine. Not only did he toss my trunk in the middle of the street, he had so little concern for me that he left me standing all alone, even though it was obvious no one was awaiting my arrival."

"How awful for you." Camie popped a strip of bacon into a biscuit and took a small bite out of it. "But it turned out well. I can't believe Nathan Pierce rescued you and brought you all the way out here in the middle of the night. How romantic."

Iris's mind went back to the evening before. What more could a girl want from a man? Mr. Pierce was tall, handsome, and a perfect gentleman who had been most accommodating and helpful. He had been a model of propriety from the moment they met until he left her at the Sherers' door. And yet, when she considered her arrival, it was not his blond hair and handsome face that appeared in her mind's eye. Instead she saw a head of darker hair, a lock of which fell forward on a wide forehead. She saw a dimple and the spark of intelligence in dark eyes. She shook her head to displace the image. Maybe the reason she remembered him was because he had been the first person she'd met after her arrival.

She decided the best way to banish the troublesome image was to concentrate on finishing her breakfast and getting dressed. "Do you have a dress I can borrow until my bags get here?"

"Of course, Iris. You know that anything I have is yours, but there's no need. Mr. Pierce delivered your trunks earlier as he promised. They're sitting right outside the bedroom door." Her eyebrow arched. "I think he was disappointed that you weren't awake so you could express your appreciation in person."

Iris slid from the warmth of the bed. "I had no idea he could really get them here so quickly."

"I think that man is smitten." Camie followed her to the hall. "Nathan's parents died when he was a young boy. His uncle, Richard Pierce, raised him. They own the dry goods store in Daisy, and his uncle is also the leader of the town council. Everybody calls Mr. Pierce the mayor. He and Nathan are the richest folks for miles around. Mayor Pierce moved here a long time ago and bought up lots of land. I guess Nathan is the most eligible bachelor we have in these parts."

"You know I don't care anything about money or land-holdings." Iris opened her trunk and drew out a brown wool dress and apron. "It's a man's heart that counts."

Camie plopped back down on the bed to watch her get ready. "He seems to have a heart of gold. He came to your rescue, didn't he?"

"I guess so. I met another man last night, too." Iris pulled her dress over her head. "His name is Adam Stuart."

"Adam Stuart?" Camie made a tsking sound with her tongue. "He's a bitter, cantankerous sort. The exact opposite of Nathan."

"I see." Iris walked over to a small mirror hanging above the dressing table to consider what might be done with her hair. She frowned at her reflection. She had to agree with her friend's assessment of Mr. Stuart's personality. So why did his dimpled smile remain so clear in her memory? Was it the pain she'd seen in his eyes? The man had been drunk. His pain was probably caused from a liverish complaint.

Iris checked herself. She was determined to banish all thoughts of Adam Stuart from her mind. Focusing her attention on the wild mane that floated around her head, Iris attacked it with impatient, rapid strokes. The more she brushed, the more her hair seemed to expand.

"Here, let me." Camie stepped up behind her and took the brush from Iris's hand. With long, gentle motions, she patiently tamed the wild curls. "You have such beautiful, thick hair. I always wanted curls like these."

"And I always wanted straight blond hair like you and my ma have."

Camie pinned Iris's hair up, allowing a few ringlets to escape at the temples and the nape of her neck. "There we go. You look perfect."

Iris looked at both of their reflections in the mirror to savor the moment before turning to give Camie a hug. "You're the best friend ever. Now, can we go see Emily and Erin?"

Camie's nod was emphatic.

They tarried only long enough to make the bed and pick up the pins Iris had scattered the night before. She was relieved at how easy it was to control her thoughts. All she had to do was concentrate on the task at hand. Gathering the breakfast tray, she began quizzing Camie about the family she was going to work for.

"You will hardly see Mr. Spencer. Since his family died, Wayha busies himself with the business of his plantation. The little girls, June Adsila and Anna Hiawassee, are adorable."

"What interesting names." Iris tried to picture the little girls with long black hair and dark eyes.

"Yes. Mr. Spencer wanted his granddaughters to have English names as a sign of their right to be American citizens, but their parents also wanted them to remember their heritage so they insisted on adding traditional Cherokee names."

"I see. Were they difficult to care for?"

Camie shook her head. "They were little angels. Almost too quiet. Of course they were still recovering from the loss of their parents, but I can remember wishing they would laugh and run around outside like we used to do." She stopped talking as they entered the dining room.

Iris was impressed by the size of the Sherer home. The dining room was well appointed with a large table and six chairs. Her gaze was drawn to the large window that took up most of one wall, and her mouth dropped open. The view was stunning. Although the land close to the house was flat, in the distance she could see mountains rising up toward the sky. It reminded her that she was far, far away from Nashville.

Camie allowed her a minute to absorb the view before walking through a door at the far end of the dining room. "Come in here and see our little angels."

Iris forgot all about the scenery outside. As she entered the kitchen, she caught sight of Emily and Erin, the Sherers' twins. They were playing with a wooden bowl their father must have given them, beating the bottom side of it with spoons and laughing at the noise they created. Camie plucked one of them from the floor and kissed her soundly, her blond hair a shade or two darker than the white strands on her daughter's head.

"This is Emily." She smiled widely at Iris. "And that is Erin."

"They are beautiful." Serious brown eyes looked at her, and Iris's heart melted. A pull on her skirt made her look down. Erin gazed up at her. Iris reached down and scooped her up, totally captivated by her gap-toothed smile. "I don't know how you ever get any work done." She kissed the soft cheek, delighted when Erin's arms circled her neck.

Camie nodded. "I hated to leave Wayha's children without a teacher, but you can understand why I had to."

Lance walked over and put an arm around his wife. "That's why we're so glad you could come to Daisy. Knowing that the Spencer girls are being loved and taught by a kind Christian lady is an answer to our prayers."

Iris dropped another kiss on the top of Erin's head. "It's an answer to my prayers as well."

five

Adam leaned against the bar and fingered the glass of amber liquid in front of him. He was shaking but not because of the March wind outside the tavern. When had escape become so important to him? And why did it matter? He picked up the glass and studied it. Candlelight gleamed through it, turning it golden.

"No matter how long you look at it, that whiskey is not going to turn back into corn." Margaret Coleridge, the tavern's auburn-haired singer, took the seat next to him at the bar. "I'll take a cup of coffee, Cyrus."

The bartender nodded. As the man filled a mug and placed it in front of her, Adam tipped his glass against his lips and drank its liquid down in one quick gulp. He grimaced as the bitter taste of the whiskey filled his mouth and burned its way down his throat. He lifted his chin at Cyrus, who pulled a bottle from underneath the counter and refilled his glass. This time Adam didn't hesitate. He downed the glass without studying it, anxious for the forgetfulness it promised.

"Slow down there, Adam." Margaret's green gaze studied him, as mysterious as a cat's. "You don't want to be drunk before I start my performance."

Adam smiled and patted her arm. "I've heard you before."

"Are you criticizing my talent?"

"Not at all. I've told you many times that you should go to Washington. You're too good to stay in this backwater. You'd be in great demand. Even the imperious President Jackson would be impressed."

A frown appeared on Margaret's face. "I doubt he would let me into his house when he learned that part of my heritage is Cherokee."

He tilted his head and considered her words. "Did you know that he adopted an Indian boy who was orphaned in battle?"

"Are you trying to tell me that the man who is almost solely responsible for the removal of the Cherokee Nation has an Indian son?"

Adam couldn't believe he had put himself into the position of defending the man who had ended all of his dreams. He guessed that was one of the worst things about being a lawyer—no matter which side he argued, he could see the strengths of the other. "Yes, he had an Indian son. Sadly the boy died the year before Jackson became president."

"Yet he fights against allowing Indians to control their own futures. If not for his utter disregard for the law, the Cherokee would be safe on their land."

Adam tapped his empty glass and shoved another gold coin across the counter. Cyrus obligingly refilled his drink. He tossed it back, barely feeling the burn. With a gusty sigh, he turned around on his stool and surveyed the room.

He knew most of the men by name, but he wouldn't consider any of them a friend. He was an outsider and a known Indian sympathizer. Of course, he'd done little to encourage friendliness since his arrival in Daisy. The last man he'd been close to, his business partner, had betrayed him in the worst way. It was far easier to maintain some distance. That way he wouldn't get hurt. . .again.

All the regulars were here, some awaiting Margaret's performance while others played games of chance. It was the same every night. At one time Adam would not have joined them. But lately he felt that he fully understood

Solomon's cynical suggestion to eat, drink, and be merry. No one watched out for the poor and downtrodden. Regardless of what they taught over at Brainerd Mission, he could detect no master plan. He grimaced at the bitter certainty that filled his heart. *Because there was no Master.* All of them were simply living here. Heaven and hell? Who really knew what would happen when this life ended?

Margaret put a hand on his arm. "I hope you defeat the demons chasing you, Adam." She stood and headed toward the raised stage where she performed nightly.

A couple of years ago pioneers had left a piano behind, likely trading it for supplies to see them through their journey southward. Adam wondered what the family would think if they could see it sitting in this tavern. He shrugged. Given the dangers of the trail, they'd likely died or been killed before they reached their destination. Such was the way of this world.

The men clapped and called out to Margaret, but she walked past them without a glance to the left or right. When she reached the platform, she nodded to the piano player and turned to smile at the audience, her dark gaze piercing him from across the room.

Adam leaned back against the bar and watched her sing, his foggy mind still able to appreciate the talent she displayed. A disturbance at the door drew his attention. "Our fine mayor has decided to join us tonight," he said to no one in particular.

Richard Pierce ran a thumb down the length of his suspenders and surveyed the room, a sneer evident on his face. Adam raised one eyebrow. If the man disliked the tavern, why didn't he stay home like the other "righteous citizens" of Daisy? Adam didn't disturb their Sunday morning church services, so why should they come bother him at his chosen haunt?

"If you're looking for Nathan"—Adam gestured at the rowdy crowd—"he hasn't graced us tonight." Now that he thought of it, it was odd that Nathan was absent. He was usually present to watch Margaret sing, even though he didn't drink or gamble.

"Actually, I'm looking for you." The elder Mr. Pierce shook his head at a barmaid headed his way. She shrugged and turned her smiling attention to another customer.

"I'll have the council's transcription ready in a day or two," Adam growled. His job as the town scribe was what paid for his evenings, but he was tired of everyone pushing him to finish his work. It wasn't as though anything earthshaking had happened at the council meeting. It was always the same—the council discussed ways to attract more settlers, or they complained because the Indians were encroaching in some way on their rights. Ha! Those same men had no trouble trading at Ross's Landing on the far side of the river, the settlement that had been founded by John Ross, the chieftain of the Cherokee Nation. He wished Ross would come home where he belonged instead of fighting the lost cause in Washington. Then they could spend their time protecting the people who lived here. And Adam wouldn't have to deal with the likes of the pompous windbag standing next to him.

"No, I need to hire your services."

What an odd development. Adam straightened the collar of his shirt in an attempt to appear more professional. "What's the problem?"

"Some thieving Indians have been stealing my livestock."

Disgust filled him. Adam should have known better than to hope for a real job, a chance to be an advocate. He slouched forward again. "Sounds like you need the sheriff more than an attorney. Or maybe a gunman to teach the rustlers to respect your property."

The mayor pulled out his watch and glanced at it before answering. "You misunderstand me, Mr. Stuart. I need someone to get a copy of that treaty from Washington. It's time these Indians understood that this town is going to be run by white men."

"I can't help you." Adam tried to keep his voice neutral, but it was hard. He couldn't abide the prejudice that had been unleashed since news of the treaty had leaked out. It might be true that the American government was going to remove the Indians from their rightful land and that some of the Cherokee had turned traitor to their own people and signed the treaty, but he didn't have to support their efforts.

"You mean you *won't* help me." The mayor spat at the floor, barely missing Adam's foot.

Anger burned white-hot in Adam's chest. His fist clenched. He'd like nothing better than to plant it in the smug countenance of Richard Pierce. Then sanity returned. He was no Arthurian knight with a sacred quest. No, he had more in common with Don Quixote, the poor deluded man who tilted at windmills. Adam knew he was nothing but a broken shell of a man waiting for his life to end. "Whether I cannot or will not doesn't matter. What matters is that you need to find someone else."

"You're a sorry excuse for a man, even by lawyers' standards." The man's voice was soft and venomous. "I must have been crazy to think you'd like to earn a respectable salary. Do you think anyone else is going to hire you? Where do you think you'll end up if you don't take this job?"

"I guess I'll end up dead whether I work or not." Adam hunched a shoulder. "The same as you."

Pierce huffed once or twice before leaving him alone.

Adam concentrated on his glass. His head was beginning

to ache, a sure sign that the past was trying to resurrect itself in his mind. He took another gulp and waited for his memory to recede.

Margaret had finished singing when he struggled up from his stool. Adam made uneven progress across the tavern floor, pushing through the door and taking a deep breath. He smiled as he thought of the tall woman with flyaway hair who'd been stranded right here a week earlier. She'd looked so lost and abandoned, like a puppy looking for someone to feed and care for it. Some sentimental part of him had surfaced briefly that night, wanting to protect her and make sure nothing destroyed the innocence in her gaze. But she'd accepted Nathan's offer of help, instead. *Smart girl.* Adam wondered if it was the alcohol that had made her appear so beautiful and pure. *Most likely.*

Adam banished thoughts of her from his mind and concentrated on keeping his gait even, a challenge ever since he'd been attacked and left for dead after the treaty signing in New Echota. Although the pain in his leg didn't trouble him when he was drinking, his ability to walk suffered greatly. But he didn't have far to go. His office, one of the few commercial buildings on the main street of Daisy, was only a few feet away.

Opening the door, he shuffled past a large oak desk. A second door took him to his apartment, the room where he slept and ate. Had he locked the front door? He shrugged. He was safe even if the door was standing open. Who would want to disturb a broken-down lawyer with no future and too much past?

With a grunt, he removed his coat, boots, and pistol before falling into bed and embracing oblivion.

six

"Tell me about the Spencer family." Iris glanced at Lance, wishing Camie had been able to come with them this morning. But that was selfish on her part. Camie was at home, caring for her daughters. Little Erin had a cough, and Camie had not wanted to risk the croup.

The cold air nipped at her cheeks and made her thankful for the thick fur that covered her legs. This part of Tennessee was so different from home. Instead of gentle hills dotted with farms and streams, the ground rose up and reached for the clouds scuttling across the sky.

Lance guided the wagon down a slope toward the river that bisected the valley and formed a natural barrier between Indian land and American soil. "Well, you already know he's a Cherokee. He moved to this area before it was Hamilton County and built a home on land granted to him by the state of North Carolina. He had one daughter, who married and had two little girls, June and Anna." He paused and looked at Iris. "Everything seemed to be going well for the family until Mr. Spencer's wife, daughter, and son-in-law died."

She met his gaze, unsurprised by the empathy she saw in it. "What happened?"

"Cholera."

Iris's eyes closed briefly. The word brought nightmare images of sickness and death. An outbreak of cholera had swept through Nashville last year, leaving many dead in its wake. Iris's heart ached for the family. "What a blessing the little girls didn't die."

"They stayed home with the house slave while Spencer took the others to the village on Lookout Mountain where they became ill, not knowing that the disease was spreading through the Cherokee tribe. He was the only one who came back."

"Those poor little girls." Her eyes filled with tears as Iris considered what it would have been like to lose her ma and pa so suddenly. "How old were they?"

"Anna was just a baby, and her sister was about two."

"They probably don't even remember their ma." She turned to Lance. "It must have been hard on Camie to have to stop caring for them."

"Yes it was. She was so glad when your parents wrote to us."

Iris looked about for another topic of conversation. "Does that mountain have a name?"

"That's Lookout Mountain. It's the tallest peak in this part of the world."

It reminded her of a cantankerous old man with hunched shoulders, and the leafless trees scattered across its summit made the peak appear to be his balding head. "How far away is it?"

Lance's eyes narrowed as he calculated the distance. "It's probably ten miles."

"It looks much closer."

"I suppose so." He smiled at her. "Since you're from Nashville, the mountains must be quite different to you."

Iris leaned against the back of the wagon seat and breathed deeply. "I like it here though."

This morning, once Lance had loaded her things into the wagon, she and Camie had tearfully hugged each other. As they pulled out onto the road, Iris had been torn by conflicting emotions. Part of her wanted to stay with her childhood friend for a few more days, but another part of her was anxious to begin her new position. Now that she had heard the story of the Spencer children, she was glad she had not tarried longer. The Spencer children needed someone to hold them and love them.

"Camie is so happy to have you living close by. I hope you will be able to visit often." Lance's words brought her thoughts back to him.

"It's wonderful to see her so hap—" The word broke off when her mouth formed an O as they drove through an iron gate onto the Spencer estate. Thick woods had hidden the large home until they turned into the lane. It was more a mansion than a house. She'd never seen such a large home except in some of the fancier neighborhoods of Nashville. It was made of dark red brick and resembled a large box. . .a very large box.

As they drew closer, she saw the house had three floors. A row of windows at ground level indicated the presence of a basement, too. Dormer windows jutted out from the sloping, gray-tiled roof that made up the third floor. Four windows per floor looked out on one side, lined up one on top of the other with symmetrical precision. The front side of the home featured a porch on the first floor, topped by an identical balcony for the second floor, each flanked by six white columns. The dark-paneled double doors that formed the entrance on the first floor were echoed by an identical doorway on the second floor. The third floor had no door or balcony, but six windows completed the balanced architecture of the house.

Iris focused on the second-floor balcony, wondering what room led to it and hoping it would be the children's parlor. Once the temperature warmed a bit, she could see herself teaching the two little girls while they sat on the balcony and listened to the cheerful gurgle of the nearby stream that wound a silvery path along one side of the property.

Lance slowed the wagon as they reached the wide set of stairs marching up to the front porch, while Iris admired the beaded detail on woodwork that separated the brick walls from the tiled roof. She hadn't realized until now just how wealthy Mr. Spencer must be.

Iris accepted Lance's help to dismount and trailed him up to the front door. He grabbed an ornate brass knocker and banged it against the polished wood of the wide front door to announce their arrival.

After a moment the door opened, and a short, rotund woman with a face as dark as a starless night wrung her hands on a white apron and smiled at them. Her white teeth shone brightly in a face wreathed with smiles. "If it isn't Master Lance come to visit." She turned her dark brown gaze to Iris. "And you must be the new nanny. I have to say it's a relief to see you. Not that I don't adore the children, but there's so much other work that needs to be done."

Iris felt a little overwhelmed as the friendly woman continued her monologue. Uncertain what else to do, she gathered her skirts and dropped a curtsy.

"Oh, you don't need to be bowing to me, missy. It's not like I'm kin to the master. I just keep the house and watch over the children."

Lance greeted the older woman. "Josephine, it's good to see you."

"Who's here?"

Josephine peered back over her shoulder. "It's Master Sherer and the new nanny."

Iris looked past her to the man who was making his slow way across the marble floor of the vestibule. His hair was mostly gray, although she could see a few strands that were as black as a raven's wings. He wore it parted in the middle and pulled back in a neat queue, which had the effect of making him look very old-fashioned. Most of the men she knew had shorter haircuts that did not have to be tied back. Mr. Spencer used a cane carved from black walnut that made her think of the one Grandpa Taylor had made for her grandma.

A wave of homesickness struck her as suddenly as a bolt of lightning. For a moment she desperately yearned to visit her grandparents' farm. She closed her eyes for a second and took a deep breath.

What nonsense! She was here because it was her dream. She opened her eyes, smiled brightly, and held out her hand to her new employer. "It's a pleasure to meet you, Mr. Spencer."

He moved his cane to his left hand and took her hand in his. "Many prayers have been answered by your safe arrival." His face was weathered, and his nose was broad and slightly crooked, as though it had been broken sometime in the past. His eyes were faded brown in color, but they held an expression of welcome that eased fears Iris hadn't even realized she held.

"Thank you, Mr. Spencer. I am thankful to be here."

"Perhaps you shouldn't be quite so thankful, Miss Landon."

Iris squinted in the direction from which Mr. Spencer had come. A man stood in the doorway, but she couldn't see his features because of the sunlight streaming into the vestibule from the room behind him. She could see that he was tall and slender, but he didn't look at all familiar to her. How did he know her name?

"Don't pay any attention to Mr. Stuart." Her host frowned over his shoulder at the man. "He is filled with doom and gloom today."

Iris looked back toward the man in the doorway. Mr. Stuart?

The man who had knocked her down on the night of her arrival? She barely heard Lance's greeting as she remembered that evening.

Mr. Stuart looked completely different when he was not inebriated. His light brown hair had been styled so that it no longer fell over his forehead, and his clothing was neither wilted nor creased. He stood much straighter, too. The only thing she did not like about his transformation was the stern look on his face and the disappearance of his dimples. His mouth had a distinctive downturn, and his brows were drawn together in a frown. How had she ever thought him charming or genial?

She turned her attention back to Lance. "Thank you so much for bringing me. I will come to visit as soon as I may."

"We'll look forward to it, Iris. You know that Camie and I are thrilled to have you so close." He nodded to the older man. "I suppose we'll see all of you again soon."

Iris tried to ignore the snort from Mr. Stuart as she assured Lance that she hoped to see him and his family at church. She glanced at Mr. Stuart. From his raised chin and downturned lips to the way he cast his gaze to the ceiling, he personified disdain. Did the man not even attend the local church? What an awful thing. She could not imagine trying to get through the week without the chance to join other Christians in worship and fellowship.

A little voice inside her head stopped Iris's thoughts. Was she being judgmental? Perhaps Mr. Stuart attended services across the river at Brainerd Mission or in some other community. Perhaps he had a sweetheart who lived nearby, and he chose to attend her church's services. A disagreeable feeling fluttered through her stomach, and Iris wondered if she was coming down with a cold. She hoped not. She didn't want anything to mar her first days with her new charges.

As she followed Josephine upstairs to the nursery, she heard Mr. Spencer invite Lance in for a business discussion. She wondered if their business would change the expression on Adam Stuart's face.

❧

Adam watched as the young woman gathered up her skirts and followed the house slave up the wide stairs to the nursery. He could not believe anyone of Miss Iris Landon's ilk would make a decent nanny, but he supposed Spencer had his reasons for hiring someone so young, inexperienced. . .and beautiful. She was nearly as tall as he and carried herself with the assurance of European royalty. And her puppy-brown eyes had been filled with innocence and hopeful expectation. She had absolutely nothing in common with the nanny who had raised him and his siblings. That woman had been older and much more fierce than he imagined Miss Landon could ever force herself to be. She reminded him more of Sylvia Sumner.

Sylvia. The name provoked a stabbing pain in his chest. It made him want a drink, but he couldn't leave. Not when work remained to be done.

Adam followed Lance and Mr. Spencer into the parlor, but a trill of laughter floating down from the upstairs landing made him want to run from the house before he made a fool of himself. He could clearly recall meeting Miss Iris Landon when she'd been dropped off in front of Poe's Tavern in the middle of the night. He had been drawn to her natural beauty even then. He could try to convince himself that it wasn't true, but something about Iris Landon made her stand out from other women. Some undaunted spirit that called to him. So he'd paid attention to what was being said about her in town.

Nathan Pierce had been the first to report on Miss Iris

Landon, describing her as "that pretty, curly-haired gal staying with the Sherers." Then Adam had heard she would be moving into the Spencer household as nanny to the two little orphaned Indian girls since Camie Sherer had given up the job.

A maelstrom of discussion had taken over as the community discussed whether or not a marriageable white woman should work in an Indian household. That brought forth those who had originally been against the Indian children being cared for by Camie Sherer. Hadn't they tried to warn people at the time that no good would come of accepting Wayha Spencer's decision to hire a non-Indian female to tend his granddaughters?

It was all a part of what was wrong with this country. Adam didn't know why it still irritated him to hear the biased comments of the white settlers. He should have learned by now that the original inhabitants of this land would never be accepted as equals. Not when acceptance meant that thousands of acres of land would be unavailable to white settlers.

Miss Iris Landon's willingness to work for an Indian family notwithstanding, most white people only wanted to exploit Indians or have them removed to some inhospitable land far away. He didn't know which was worse, the greedy landgrabbers or the overeager missionaries. Miss Landon was definitely not part of the first group. She had most likely accepted her position so she could proselytize the little girls. Like most women, she had an ability to deceive herself into believing in a benevolent Creator, but why must she try to force her beliefs on others?

"You're not making your case very well." Mr. Spencer's sharp gaze brought Adam to the matter at hand. He waved Adam to a horsehair-covered settee before taking a seat in an overstuffed chair to one side of the hearth. He pointed Lance to a straight-backed chair that stood between his seat and Adam's.

"I apologize, sir. What more do you need to hear?" Adam had been all through this many times before, but he was willing to explain it again if Mr. Spencer wanted him to. All he needed to do was focus on the reason he'd come out here in the first place, a reason that had nothing to do with what was going on upstairs.

"Adam here feels I should put my house and lands up for sale."

Lance looked in his direction, and Adam could feel his ire rising in response to the man's incredulity. "It's not like I'm the one who wants to buy it. I've never pretended to have that kind of money at my disposal."

"Then why do you advise Mr. Spencer to sell? In spite of the tragedy of losing his loved ones, there is no reason he should move back to Lookout Mountain."

"Of course not. That's an outlandish idea!" Adam tugged at his waistcoat and straightened his back. "Who said anything about his going to the village?"

"You don't understand, Lance." Mr. Spencer tapped his cane on the floor to get their attention. "Adam thinks I should go to the new Indian Territory."

"What!" Lance turned to Adam. He looked confused. "I thought you were an opponent of Indian removal. I thought you believed as I do that the Indians have a right to their land."

Adam shrugged and looked out the window as he tried to organize his thoughts. How could these men be so blind to the truth? It was time to face facts. President Jackson had won. It didn't matter what they or anyone else thought. The Cherokee would never be allowed to stay in Tennessee. If he could convince his friend of that truth, then the old man would be able to see the logic in moving now—he would have his choice of homesteads in the new Indian Territory. Instead of waiting until his home and land were wrested from him by the full force of the American government, he could sell his holdings for a reasonable amount and have money when he made the move. "What I *believe* has no bearing on it. The fact is that the signing of the treaty at New Echota is a death knell to the Cherokee Nation."

"If that were the case, Chief Ross would be here gathering his belongings instead of staying in Washington." Lance's voice was calm and reasonable, but to Adam it reeked of ignorance and self-deceit. "Obviously he believes there is still a chance for the Cherokee to win."

"Again that word—believe." Adam's jaw was so tight it ached. "It sounds to me like that missionary wife of yours has turned your brain into mush."

Lance came out of his chair like a shot. "Be careful what you say about my wife, sir."

Adam also stood and sized up the shorter man in case he had to defend himself. Lance Sherer looked brawny and strong, a side effect of earning his living traipsing through the wilderness to survey property. But no matter the outcome of a bout of fisticuffs, Adam knew he had to apologize. He'd allowed his temper to get the better of him. He let his gaze drop. "I meant no disrespect."

The tension in the room did not ease appreciably. He could see the other man's hands still clenched in fists.

After a moment Mr. Spencer sighed, pulled himself out of his chair, and came to stand between them. He turned his back on Adam and addressed Lance. "As a good Christian, you will no doubt accept his apology."

Adam spread his hands. "I'm really sorry. This is a difficult time for all of us."

Lance nodded and turned back to his chair. "What do you need from me?" He directed his question to Mr. Spencer.

The older man went to the mantel and grabbed a large wooden box from it. Adam watched as Mr. Spencer maneuvered his way to the settee and sat heavily. He opened the box, and Adam saw that it contained several official documents. "Even if you're right and the Indians are forced to leave their homes, I am in a different situation. I hold an official warrant for this land." He triumphantly pulled out a parchment and waved it.

"That warrant is only a piece of paper." Adam could not keep the mockery out of his voice. "If the people who want your land set fire to this house, what would you have?"

"That is why I invited Lance into our conversation. It seems to me that his arrival could be considered God's intervention. He can keep the deed safe for me."

Adam mulled over the idea. Letting a third party hold the warranty was a good idea. He knew that Lance kept warranties of properties he surveyed, but since he had never surveyed Mr. Spencer's land, no one would suspect where the official deed was being held. He nodded his agreement. "But I still think you'd be better advised to leave while you still have a choice."

"I will raise my granddaughters in this home I built until the government of the United States forces me out."

Adam shrugged. Why should he care what happened? He should never have come in the first place. Obviously no one else had the vision to see the future that was bearing down on them.

❧

As she climbed the stairwell behind the house slave, Iris soaked up the atmosphere of the Spencer home. It did not feel much like an Indian home—at least not the Indian homes she had visited at the side of her parents. No stretched skins or animal horns hung on the walls. She saw framed oil paintings rather than charcoal drawings. The draperies were constructed of rich burgundy velvet, and she noticed a pair of vases made of etched glass. How beautiful they would be when filled with fresh spring flowers.

Josephine opened a door at the top of the landing, and both of them entered the children's parlor. It was a handsomely apportioned room, light and airy, and filled with a profusion of toys for young children. Iris clapped her hands as she looked around. It was a child's dream come true. She could imagine playing in this room as a little girl. What fun she and her friends would have had. She noticed a checkerboard and its black and red pieces, a box of marbles, several spinning tops, and a whole shelf of dolls. Some of the dolls were hand-made cornstalk dolls like the ones she'd had as a little girl, but there were also several fancy dolls with porcelain faces and intricate dresses.

"Where are the children?" Iris asked once she could pull her gaze from the wall of toys.

Josephine winked at her. "They love to hide from me. I spend a large part of my day trying to discover all their hidey-holes."

A faint giggle came to her ears. Iris realized this must be a game for the girls and Josephine.

"Now where could they be this time?" Josephine put a finger on her chin and looked around. "I wonder if they're on the porch." She swept across the room and pulled the doors open, sticking her head outside and looking from left to right.

"Are they out there?" Iris joined the game.

"No luck today." Josephine came back inside. "You know, one day I found them in the secret shelf Mr. Spencer had built underneath the window seats. I wonder if that's where they're hiding today."

She advanced on the window seats. Suddenly the giggles stopped. "Yes indeed." She opened the window seats with a flourish.

Two dark heads popped up. Two mouths shrieked. Josephine threw her hands up in the air, and Iris laughed as hard as she had since her arrival in this part of Tennessee. It took several moments for all of them to calm down enough to talk.

"Come out, girls, and meet your new nanny."

A slight hesitation preceded the girls climbing out of the window seats and coming to where Iris still stood in the center of the room. She could see how much they depended on each other by the way their hands clung together. The younger child hung back slightly and plopped a thumb in her mouth. They both looked up at Iris, their big brown eyes filled with a mixture of trepidation and curiosity.

The nervousness Iris had felt upon her arrival melted away. These little girls were adorable. She could hardly wait to hold them in her arms. She knelt in front of them and smiled. "You cannot believe how badly I've wanted to see the two of you." She looked at the older sister. "You must be June."

A hesitant nod answered her.

Iris turned to the younger girl. "Now don't tell me. . . ." She put a finger on her chin and looked upward as though trying to think. "Your name is Amber?"

A headshake from both girls.

Iris tapped her chin. "Elsie? Laura? Ada?" At each guess, the girls shook their heads. "Maybe you'd better tell me then, or I might spend all day guessing."

As Iris had hoped, the younger child removed her thumb to answer. "Anna Hi'wa'se." She had a little trouble with the vowels in her Cherokee name.

"What a pretty name," Iris encouraged, eliciting a smile.

The older girl took a step forward. "I'm June Adsila."

Iris nodded. "That's a pretty name, too."

"*Adsila* is Cherokee for 'blossom.'" The older child offered the information as though seeking Iris's approval. "*Hiawassee* means 'meadow.'"

"Well, isn't that grand?" Iris laughed and lowered her voice as though she had a secret to tell them. "My name is Iris. Do you know what an iris is?" She waited while they glanced at each other. They shook their heads in unison. "An iris is a type of flower that has a pretty purple blossom and can be seen in the meadow in the spring."

"Our ma is in heaven." Anna made the statement before returning her thumb to her mouth.

Iris prayed for the right answer to give the girls. They were both watching her, their brown eyes inscrutable. "That's right. And I know she is proud she has two such beautiful young ladies here to keep their grandpa company."

"That's what I tell them all the time." Josephine reentered the conversation, warm approval evident in her voice.

Iris stood and brushed her skirts, although the floor was too spotless to have soiled it. She wanted nothing more than to wrap her arms around the precious girls who were watching her. She was so grateful to be here and sent a quick prayer of thanksgiving heavenward.

"Why don't you come with me, girls? We'll let Miss Iris unpack, and then she can join us." She glanced quizzically at Iris. "Can you be ready in an hour? I will need to get started on the day's chores by then."

"I don't think that's necessary." Iris smiled down at June and Anna. "Would the two of you like to come with me? I could use some help unpacking."

Two nods answered her. The girls turned pleading looks

on Josephine, who held up her hands and laughed. "An extra hour to get more work done? That would be a great help, Miss Iris, if you're sure."

"Of course I'm sure. Maybe the girls can also give me a tour of the house. I'm sure they know every nook and cranny of their beautiful home."

"What a good idea. Then you can all come down to the kitchen. I'll make sure Cook has a snack all ready for you." Josephine disappeared down the hall with a wave of her hand.

Iris looked down. "Oh, my. I forgot to ask Miss Josephine where my room is. Do you think the two of you can help me find it?"

They glanced at each other before nodding. She held out her hands. June grabbed her left while Anna reached for the right one. Then they tugged her around and out the doorway. She had to laugh at their eagerness. This was going to be an easier job than she had ever imagined.

seven

Iris sighed as she tried to tame her hair. It was raining outside, bad news for two reasons. The first and least important was her unruly hair. The second was the disappointment her girls would face when they found that their planned picnic would have to be postponed. She pulled her hair back and wrestled a ribbon around it.

In the week since her arrival, she had grown to love the sweet Spencer girls. And they had responded to her with all the love in their dear little hearts. A clap of thunder brought another sigh. It looked like a picnic was out of the question. She wrinkled her nose at her reflection in the mirror. She didn't look overly professional, but she had learned during the past week that she would most likely not see anyone but her charges and the slaves.

She still found it hard to believe that Mr. Spencer had a house full of slaves. How could a man own slaves when his own people were fighting a battle for the right to control their futures? She understood his desire to live like his white counterparts, but not all wealthy men had slaves to work in their fields and keep their homes clean. Her pa was a good example. When it came time to plant or harvest his crops, he employed workers and paid them a fair wage. Their house was not so large that she, Ma, and Hannah could not keep up with the housework. But if it got to be too much work, she knew her parents would hire a housekeeper, not purchase a human being to do the work.

She had discovered the truth at the end of her first day.

After meeting June Adsila and Anna Hiawassee, who were the sweetest little girls she could have imagined, Iris had asked Josephine how the staff managed their days off. She had neglected to ask her employer if she would be allowed to attend Sunday services in town and still take an afternoon off to visit the Sherers. Josephine had shrugged her shoulders and explained that she did not take days off except for Christmas as she was a slave. Iris had been incredulous, but Josephine had assured her that she was happy to find herself in a good home with a kind master.

Iris wanted to ask Mr. Spencer why he owned slaves, but she had not seen the man since the day of her arrival. He had sent for his granddaughters once or twice, but she was not included in the invitations. So she had spent the time describing her new home and situation to her family in a letter. Perhaps the good Lord would provide an opportunity later. She hoped He would also provide her with the words to present her case to the man.

A knock on the door was her signal that the girls were awake and ready to be dressed. Her room was in the center of a connected suite, with June's bed in one room while her little sister's was located in the other. It was yet another indication of the wealth enjoyed by the Spencer family. A room for each of the children was a luxury where she came from. Of course, little Anna could often be discovered in June's bed by morning. An arrangement that neither girl seemed to mind.

Iris opened her door and was immediately bombarded as June and Anna barreled into her for early morning hugs. "Good morning. Who is ready for breakfast?"

"When can we go on our pickanick?" June asked.

"Weeell," Iris drew the word out as she kissed first one child and then the other, "it seems that God has other plans in mind for us today."

"I told you so." Little Anna might be younger, but she was the more talkative and logical of the pair.

June's eyes filled with tears.

"Don't worry, little one. We will go on the next pretty day." She walked into June's room and pulled a shift from her bureau, laying it across the bed. The next hour was filled with questions and exclamations as she got the girls dressed and seated in their parlor where they would break their fasts together.

The mouthwatering smells of crisp bacon and warm bread greeted them. Iris helped the girls fill their plates before choosing a warm biscuit and coddled eggs for herself. "Whose turn is it to bless our food this morning?"

"It's June's turn," precocious Anna answered as usual. She glanced at her sister. "But I don't think she wants to talk to God today."

"Is that true, June?"

The older sister stared at her plate but nodded her agreement.

Anna was unperturbed by her sister's silence. "Do you want me to say the blessing?"

Iris considered the two girls, so much alike in looks, so different in personalities. June was a sweet-hearted little girl, but she obviously still grieved for her parents. Anna, on the other hand, had been much too young to remember her ma and pa, so she didn't feel the lack. "I think maybe we should talk to June about why she is so reluctant."

June shrugged.

Anna opened her mouth to answer for her sister, but Iris stopped her with a raised finger. "Let's let June tell us what is wrong."

They waited in silence as the food cooled on their plates. Finally June looked up. "Does God love us?"

Iris felt like she'd been punched in the stomach. "Of course

He loves us. Whatever would make you think otherwise?"

"Why does He make people go to heaven and leave us?"

Iris pushed her chair back and went to kneel next to June, praying for the right words to share God's love with them. "I know you miss your ma and pa so much. I miss mine, too."

June's eyes turned into brown pools of tears. "Did Jesus take them to heaven, too?"

"No, but they live far, far away from here." Iris could feel the burn of tears in her own eyes. She needed to change the tone in the nursery, or it was going to be a miserable day for all three of them. "Do you know the story about the missing sheep?"

June and Anna both shook their heads.

"Once upon a time, a boy had the job of watching over a whole flock of sheep. There were white ones and black ones and even a few spotted sheep."

"Were there any lambs?" Anna interrupted.

"Yes, Anna. Lots of lambs. Well, one day when the shepherd was counting all of his sheep, he realized that one of the baby sheep was missing. He looked in the valleys and on top of the hills, but he couldn't find the little baby sheep."

"Oh no." June's tender heart was obviously hurting for the lost sheep. "What did the boy do?"

"He left all of his other sheep in a safe place and went to find the little lost sheep. He looked and he looked until he finally found it." Iris hoped her improvisation of the scripture in Matthew was acceptable to God. Jesus didn't tell exactly how the shepherd had found his sheep, but she was certain he would have looked high and low.

"One time, one of our calves got stuck between two big rocks." Anna lifted her arms up high to show the size of the boulders. "And it took Grandpa and two other men to get it out."

"That may be what happened to the baby sheep. Or maybe

he just wandered off and couldn't find his way back home. But anyway, the shepherd boy found the baby sheep, picked it up, put it on his shoulders, and took it back home with him. He was so happy that he had found the baby sheep." Iris hugged June close. "That's because that shepherd boy loved his sheep the same way that Jesus loves you and me. That's why I'm here now. To hug you and take care of you—"

"And make sure we don't get caught in any rocks." Ever the practical one, Anna interjected her thoughts.

"That's right." Iris hugged June first then Anna. "I'll make sure you two get out of any tight spots."

Their smiles warmed Iris's heart. She stood up and returned to her chair. "How about if I say grace this morning since I feel extra thankful to get to watch out for two smart little girls?"

They nodded their acceptance. The three of them held hands. The girls bowed their heads, and Iris followed their example. "Lord, thank You for giving us this special day together. Thank You for watching out for all the lost sheep, and help us to be good shepherds with each other. Bless the hands of those who prepared this food. May it nourish our bodies in the way You nourish our souls. Amen."

Anna and June began to eat their food, but Iris only picked at her eggs and biscuit. She wanted to make this day special even if they could not go outside for a picnic. She looked around the room for inspiration. Several framed landscape paintings—some depicted mountainous terrain while others portrayed springtime meadows—decorated the walls. One in particular had become her favorite as it reminded her of Ma's garden back home. The artist had created a profusion of colorful flowers, including Iris's namesake. Inspiration struck, and joy filled her heart. "I know what we can do today."

"What?" June's voice held a note of hope that had been missing earlier.

"We'll have our picnic right here."

"But"—Anna looked around the room—"that's not a picnic. It's just a luncheon like we have every day."

Iris shook her head. "Not if we spend the morning decorating. As soon as we finish eating, we'll get out those watercolors and start painting flowers and trees. By the time we get done, you won't be able to tell we're still inside."

Dismay turned to anticipation as both girls finished their breakfasts quickly and urged Iris to hurry so they could begin their art project. After securing aprons from Josephine to protect their clothing, they excitedly returned to their parlor and looked to Iris for guidance.

Four hours later their aprons were liberally splattered with the colors of the rainbow. It had been a little slow at first, but Iris had shown them how to paint trees and flowers on their canvases. While their artwork would never capture the eye of a collector, the canvases were filled with bright swaths of color that seemed to brighten the dreary day.

Josephine had prepared a basket of food and helped them move the table to one corner of the room. They spread a blanket on the floor and sat in the middle of it while they munched on fresh cheese and bread.

"Anna, you may be outside in the middle of nowhere, but young ladies must still wipe away their food with napkins, not their sleeves." Iris's statement elicited giggles from both girls, and she smiled when the younger complied.

"Which painting is your favorite?" asked June.

"I don't know. They are all very pretty."

Anna stood up and walked over to one her sister had painted of a meadow ringed by mountains. "I like this one. It's the same as my Indian name."

"That's right, Anna. And wasn't June smart to think of painting something special for you?" Iris smiled at June, relieved to see that her sadness had been replaced by a look of satisfaction. "And I especially like the flowers you put in your picture. They look just like the irises that grow wild in the meadows at home."

"Do you like my river picture?" Anna wandered to a canvas that looked to Iris like a mishmash of greens and blues.

"Yes, it's very nice." She pointed to a dark blob on one side of the blue slash that was apparently Anna's idea of the Tennessee River. "What is that?"

"It's a fish. There are lots of fish in the river."

Iris tilted her head. She nodded. "I see it now. My goodness, what a great big fish. Big enough to feed this family for a week."

Anna nodded. She came back to the blanket and sat down. "I wish we were really outside though. Then we could find some real irises and give them to you."

"I have a secret for you, Anna. And for you, too, June."

Both girls leaned toward her. "What's your secret?" they asked in unison.

"No bouquet of flowers could be more beautiful to me than the two of you. You're the most precious bouquet any nanny could ever want." She held out her arms and gathered them close, so thankful for their loving arms and enthusiastic kisses.

eight

"They are adorable." Iris kept her voice low to avoid waking Camie's sleeping children. "They look like little angels." She watched as Camie tucked the cover more securely around her daughters and thought about how nice it would be to have children of her own.

Happiness and anticipation made her stomach flutter as she followed her friend out of the bedroom. Nathan would be here soon to have dinner with her and the Sherers. She wondered if he was the man God wanted her to marry. He was certainly nice. She was looking forward to getting to know him better.

Camie's voice interrupted her musings. "Lance and I are going to take the girls to Brainerd Mission for Easter to see Ma and Pa. We'd love for you to join us."

"I'd love to! I'm sure Mr. Spencer wouldn't mind if I took the day off."

"Good. I know how much Ma and Pa would like to see you. They were so excited when you agreed to come."

"Me, too." Iris squeezed Camie's hand. "You know that I consider your father's letter an answer to prayer."

Camie's reply was halted by a knock at the front door. "That must be Nathan and Mr. Pierce."

Iris wondered why Mrs. Pierce was not attending and made a note to ask if Nathan's aunt was ill. She smoothed her collar with nervous fingers as the Pierce gentlemen entered the parlor. A flurry of greetings and introductions filled the room.

Nathan Pierce was as nice as she remembered, but his uncle was another matter entirely. Looking from one to the other, she wondered how Nathan could be so unassuming and have a relative who practically oozed self-importance.

Although the elder Mr. Pierce was much shorter than Nathan, she could see some family resemblance. They both shared the same cornflower blue eyes and blond hair, although the hair of Nathan's uncle had begun to thin.

"It's too bad your wife could not come for dinner tonight, Mr. Pierce." Iris folded her hands in her lap.

He cleared his throat before answering. "She died some years ago, Miss Landon." He fastened his blue gaze on her face with some interest as though he was considering whether she would be an acceptable replacement.

"That is a shame. I'm sorry for your loss." Iris turned to Nathan. "I know your uncle must rely on you greatly to keep him company since your aunt's death."

Nathan shifted his feet. "I don't know about that. I run the store so Uncle Richard can tend to the town's business as well as keep our accounts straight."

"I see."

"You have an expressive face, Miss Landon." Mayor Pierce thrust out his chest. "I am rather an expert when it comes to reading faces, you see."

"Is that so?" She assumed what she hoped was an interested expression as the mayor droned on about the subject of wordless communicators.

She would be relieved when the Sherers joined them. Their housekeeper was visiting family in Athens, Georgia, so Lance was helping to set the table, a chore Camie had forbidden Iris to do. Iris loved her friend, but she didn't need help in finding a husband, which was obviously the reason for tonight's dinner party. She wondered if Camie intended to pair her with

Nathan or his uncle. Either way, the plan was doomed to failure. When God decided it was time, she would fall in love with a good Christian man, someone who would provide for her and their children the way Lance provided for Camie, Emily, and Erin.

Lance and Camie entered the parlor together, their hands linked. Iris could admit to herself that there would be advantages in having a husband, like the companionship and shared laughter that seemed to be a part of her friend's marriage. But she was content to wait for her own knight.

She glanced toward Nathan. He was a nice-looking man and very considerate. He nodded at something his uncle said. She could not fault his manners or his attitude toward her. He was exactly the sort of man she should be attracted to, so she determined she would keep an open mind. Perhaps she would fall in love with Nathan once she got to know him better.

"I think we're ready for you to come into the dining room." Camie sounded breathless. Iris wondered if the flush on her cheeks was caused by the preparations she had been making in the kitchen, or perhaps her husband had been stealing kisses from her as they worked. Maybe Camie's refusal to let Iris set the table had been driven by more than one consideration.

Both Nathan and his uncle approached Iris where she sat next to a console table. Iris set her teacup on the table, wondering how she should handle two escorts. The problem was solved when Camie swept forward and took Mayor Pierce by the arm. A nod to her husband had Lance leading the way to the dining room. "Mayor Pierce, Lance has been telling me all about the new fields you will be planting to our south. How exciting."

Nathan watched them for a moment before turning his

attention to her. "May I have the honor of escorting you?"

Nodding her head, Iris allowed him to draw her upward. They followed the others and found that Mayor Pierce was sitting in the place of honor to the right of his host's seat at the head of the table. Camie's seat, at the foot of the table, put her next to the doorway leading to the kitchen. As Nathan and Iris entered, she motioned them to the pair of places sitting side by side on her right.

Candles took up the center of the table, casting a golden glow on the room. They were ringed by pinecones and winter-berries, lending a festive atmosphere to the table.

Iris murmured her thanks to Nathan for seating her and turned to Camie. "Everything looks so nice. You're a wonderful housewife."

"I'm sure you will be one, too." Camie looked toward Nathan. "Don't you agree, Mr. Pierce?"

Iris blushed at his nod and picked up her fork. A banging at the front door startled her.

She looked at Camie, who shook her head, indicating she had no idea who was visiting at this late hour. Iris hoped it was not bad news.

Lance pushed back from the table. "Please excuse me. I imagine that's some traveler who's lost his way."

Iris was not surprised when he grabbed his rifle before heading to the front door. Unannounced visitors after dark warranted a certain degree of caution.

"Should I go with your husband?" Nathan looked at their hostess.

"Don't be foolish." His uncle answered the question. "Lance Sherer doesn't need your help to answer his door."

Iris felt sorry for Nathan. His uncle's scornful answer must have stung. Nathan was a grown man after all, not some wayward child.

She picked up her fork and watched as the elder Mr. Pierce calmly sliced a piece of meat off the roast at his elbow and put it on his plate. He was reaching for the basket of rolls when the door to the dining room burst open and slammed against the back wall.

All four diners jumped, and Iris may have even let a small cry escape her lips. She clapped a hand over her mouth to avoid waking the children upstairs and watched as Adam Stuart stumbled into the dining room, closely followed by Lance.

"I told you we are having company."

Mr. Stuart stopped. He took in the scene with a quick glance and swept a bow in Camie's general direction. "Pardon me, Mrs. Sherer, for disturbing your dinner party. I have business that cannot wait."

"Adam, what are you doing here?" asked Nathan, standing up to form a barrier between the rude man and Iris.

While she appreciated his gesture, she was not afraid of Adam Stuart. But when she would have explained her lack of fear, her words were drowned out by Adam's voice.

"I was told you'd be here." Iris watched Adam limp his way over to Nathan's uncle.

Mayor Pierce was practically cowering in his seat, apparently much more frightened by a belligerent man than he ought to be.

"Get up!" Adam raised his fists into a fighting posture.

Camie gasped.

"Leave my uncle alone." Nathan's voice was as sharp as Adam's. "If you have a problem with my family, why don't we go outside and discuss it where we won't disturb the ladies?"

Adam ignored him. "I said, get up!"

Mayor Pierce shook his head. "I will not be threatened by a drunken fool."

"I'm entirely sober and extremely angry. Is it true you called a special meeting of the council this afternoon?"

Nathan reached his uncle's side. "Why on earth are you asking such a question? Have you lost your mind?"

Although he did not rise from his chair, Mayor Pierce must have gained confidence from having his nephew close by. "Who better than the mayor to call a meeting of the council? They elected me to make those decisions."

"Everyone knows the council meets at seven o'clock on the second and fourth Monday evenings of the month." The man spat the words out as though they caused a bad taste in his mouth. "A special meeting should only be called in case of an emergency. Not because you had some sneaky idea that you wanted to shove through council before the townspeople knew anything about it."

"Do you mean to tell me that you came barging into my home and disturbed my wife and guests because the mayor called a special council meeting?" Lance frowned at Adam. "I ought to march you out of here right now."

Adam pointed a finger at Iris. "I think his special meeting had something to do with her employer. I have it on good authority that he's got a resolution ordering the immediate removal of Mr. Wayha Spencer and his family from their home and lands on this side of the river."

Iris felt her jaw drop. Her gaze went to the cowering mayor. "Is that true?"

Mayor Pierce shook his head and mopped his damp brow with one of Camie's monogrammed napkins. "Of course not! This man is jumping to conclusions based on idle speculation and gossip."

Iris turned back to Adam and spread her hands in a placating gesture. "This is obviously a misunderstanding."

Adam made a disgusted sound. "You're too naive and

trusting for your own good." He reached for Mayor Pierce's shirtfront.

Nathan grabbed his hand and pulled it back. "Don't even think about touching my uncle."

"I think we've heard enough, Mr. Stuart." Lance stepped forward and stared at Adam. "Mayor Pierce has denied your charges, so I would appreciate it if you'd leave."

A pan of frying chicken would have sizzled less than the tension in the room. Iris felt herself caught by Adam's tortured gaze. Some part of her noticed that his eyes held a green fire she'd never noticed before. She'd thought his eyes were brown, but looking into their depths, she made the discovery that the man's eyes were hazel—with enough highlights to make them appear as green as grass when he was angry.

She stared at him, for once thankful for her tall frame. He seemed to be begging her to take his part, but she couldn't do that. He had to be wrong about Mayor Pierce. Why else would he deny everything? He had to know if it was true they would all find out at the next official council meeting.

A desire came over her to smile at Mr. Stuart, offer him some comfort, however small. But it was an impossible, dim-witted idea. They were in her friend's dining room, and the man had barged in uninvited.

She watched as Lance escorted him back to the front door. Their words were muffled by the closed door of the dining room, but she could still make out Adam Stuart's angry tones in stark contrast to the calm, reasonable comments being offered by Lance.

"Shall we continue our meal?" Camie sat down and began passing the plates of food as though the recent scene had not happened.

Nathan looked toward the doorway, but he was apparently

reluctant to leave his uncle alone. Iris wondered if he thought she or Camie was a threat to the cowardly mayor. But then she grew ashamed at her thought. Knowing how kind Nathan was, he'd probably decided to stay behind so he could protect her and Camie in case Adam's visit was a ruse to cover some nefarious plot.

"He's gotten downright dangerous since the treaty signing." Mayor Pierce pulled on his collar. "We are going to have to lock him up one of these days."

"Well, it is a shame what happened to him that night." Nathan turned to Iris to explain. "He spoke out against the Ridge party, who signed the treaty at New Echota. He left and was on his way back here when he was attacked and left for dead in the middle of nowhere. A lot of men wouldn't have survived, but Adam found cover and managed to get himself back here alive. The injuries he suffered are what cause him to limp. When he came back, he got the council to hire him. He's been attending their meetings to record the minutes and to offer legal advice when he's asked to. Most of the council seems satisfied with his work." Nathan looked at his uncle, who at least had the grace to duck his head.

Iris couldn't help but admire Nathan even more as he defended the man whom he had every reason to dislike. She couldn't imagine being so charitable to anyone who tried to attack her relatives. The younger Mr. Pierce was a truly fine Christian who believed in turning the other cheek in the most trying of circumstances.

Quite the opposite of Adam Stuart. What right did he have to come bursting in on her friends? And how dare he call her naive? She had a lot of experience. Hadn't she traveled across Tennessee and been left alone in the middle of the night without any way to get to the Sherers' home? Perhaps she'd not been attacked and left for dead, but that didn't mean she was devoid of common sense.

Camie excused herself to go check on the girls and returned with a relieved smile that they had somehow slept through the commotion.

Lance returned a moment later and apologized to them for the disruption before sitting down to continue his dinner as though nothing untoward had happened.

Nathan smoothed the napkin in his lap. "I wonder why Adam Stuart came barging in here."

"He seemed to believe there will be an attempt to take Wayha Spencer's land." Lance shook his head.

"But how can that be?" asked Camie. "You showed me his origi—"

A warning shake of her husband's head stopped Camie midsentence.

Mayor Pierce shoveled food into his mouth until there wasn't a morsel left on his plate before pushing back from the table. "A fine meal, Mrs. Sherer. Please excuse me for a moment."

They continued discussing Adam Stuart's interruption and wild accusations as they lingered over Camie's delicious food.

Iris wasn't sure how much time passed before she realized Nathan's uncle had not yet returned. Had the man been grabbed by the belligerent Mr. Stuart? The thought had barely formed when Mayor Pierce pushed open the dining room door and rejoined them.

Nathan patted his stomach and sighed. "Everything was delicious."

"I'm glad you were able to enjoy the meal in spite of the interruption." Camie's smile was radiant.

"Camie is a wonderful cook." Lance's voice was as warm as his glance.

Iris added her compliments to those of the men. She was

so proud of her friend's abilities. It was obvious Camie was thriving here.

Too bad Adam Stuart was not. His accusations had been wild and unfounded. She would not let him cast a pall on her enjoyment of the evening. Instead she would concentrate on Nathan Pierce's admirable qualities.

The rest of the evening passed quickly. Iris and Camie checked on the girls once more while the men enjoyed a lively discussion about the Texas war for independence from the Mexicans. All in all, it was a pleasant evening. Iris hoped she would one day be able to be such an accomplished hostess.

nine

Iris settled herself in the wagon next to Camie before waving good-bye to June and Anna, who were clinging to Josephine's skirts. She would miss them, but Mr. Spencer had insisted they stay with him to avoid overcrowding at the Millers' home.

Lance drove to the ferryman's hut and woke him. While he arranged for their transport across the river, Iris and Camie played with Erin and Emily to keep them from fussing. A white mist hung over the river, but Iris knew it would disappear as the sun rose.

The ferryman was short and rotund with a knitted cap covering grizzled hair that matched his shaggy beard and mustache. He wore a coat of rabbit fur and long woolen socks that covered his legs all the way up to his knees. He nodded at them and headed down to the river.

Lance climbed back aboard the wagon and guided it onto the wooden raft. It only took a short time to cross the river, but Iris held her breath as she watched the swift water slide under the edge of the ferry. Lance waved to the man as he pulled the wagon back onto solid ground, and they were off on the next leg of their journey.

The sun came up over the eastern hills and brought with it some warmth. Iris found herself dozing as they made slow but steady progress on the muddy roads.

Camie's voice roused her. "Ma and Pa are going to be so excited to see you, Iris."

Iris raised an eyebrow. "I imagine they will be much more

interested in seeing their granddaughters than the child of their old friends. And rightfully so." She tickled Erin, laughing along with the girl. "You're much more interesting than an old maid nanny."

Lance's chest seemed to expand a little. "They are special, aren't they?"

"Yes they are." Iris rubbed her nose against Erin's cheek. "Children are a gift from God."

Camie pulled Emily onto her lap. "That's true, but I know my parents will be excited to see you, too."

"We're about to find out just how much." Lance turned down a lane and through a wide gate.

A large sign swung between the tall posts. "BRAINERD MISSION." Iris also read aloud the words carved into the bottom half of the sign, "So that I could but gain souls for Christ."

"It was David Brainerd's lifelong dream." Camie referred to the brave missionary whose tireless work had inspired the formation of missions like this one.

"I didn't realize how large the mission is." Iris gazed at the extensive grounds dotted with comfortable homes, livestock, and cherry orchards.

As he steered the horses, Lance pointed out the mill perched on the banks of Chickamauga Creek, as well as the main house where the students resided, and the large meetinghouse where they would attend Easter services in a little while.

"Whoa." He pulled back on the reins in front of a two-story whitewashed cabin.

Iris and Camie began gathering blankets, baskets, and children while Lance secured the horses. Before they could unload all the necessary items, the front door opened and Roman Miller, dressed in black pants and a starched shirt, stepped onto the front porch.

"They're here," he called back into the house. He had aged

somewhat, which wasn't surprising as nearly a decade had passed since Iris had last seen the man. Though his hair had turned white and his girth had widened a little, the twinkle in his dark eyes had not changed at all.

Una Miller stepped onto the front porch, wiping her hands on her apron. Her hair was pulled back in a tidy bun and was now liberally streaked with gray. Iris could see crow's feet bracketing her eyes and mouth as she smiled. It made Iris think of Ma and wonder where her family was spending their Easter Sunday. She shook off the thought. This was no time to get homesick.

Hugs from both Pastor and Mrs. Miller helped to brighten her mood. They were as excited to see her as their own grandchildren. As they went inside, Pastor Miller asked if she was happy at the Spencer home.

"Yes. June and Anna are so sweet and obedient."

"We would like to enroll them in the school here." Camie's mother led the way to the parlor, a chortling Erin in her arms. "But Mr. Spencer is adamant that they will attend school in Daisy."

Iris wandered around the parlor, admiring several charcoal sketches that decorated the walls. "He is determined for them to be treated the same as white children."

"I hope he can realize his dream," said Pastor Miller, "and that he can avoid being removed with the others." He reached for Emily as she toddled across the room. "You will enjoy having them as neighbors, won't you, little one?"

"Who is leading the service today?" asked Camie.

"I am." Her pa shifted Emily to his left arm, pulled out his pocket watch, and squinted at it. "I'd better put on my coat and tie."

Camie took Emily back. She turned to her husband, who had finished unloading the wagon. "Is there enough room for all of us to ride together?"

"That's not necessary, Camie," her ma said. "You know we usually walk to the meetinghouse."

"But the children—"

"Will be no trouble at all."

Iris nodded her agreement. After their two-hour trip in the wagon, it would be a relief to walk.

After Camie's father came back, they gathered their cloaks and set out.

Pastor Miller insisted on carrying one of his grand-daughters while his wife took the other. Camie linked one arm through her husband's and gestured for Iris to walk on her other side.

They greeted several of the other missionary families on their way to the large building where the church services would be held. The missionaries' children laughed and played with the Indian children, a sight that warmed Iris's heart. If only President Jackson could see this scene, he might understand there was no need to push for the removal of the Cherokee.

Her gaze rested for a moment on a large black horse whose tall rider stood nearby. Her heart skipped a beat. Surely she must be mistaken. Adam Stuart would not have come out here to stir up more trouble. Yet there he was. She would recognize that rumpled suit anywhere. He turned, and she caught a glimpse of his face, which he had apparently not bothered to shave. The nerve of the man. She would have walked right past him, but Pastor Miller stopped to greet him.

"I'm glad to see you here."

Adam put his hands in his coat pocket. "I am on my way to the village and thought I would stop in to say hello."

"You're just in time for our morning service." Pastor Miller turned and spotted Iris. "Come over, my dear, and meet the brightest hope of the Cherokee. Adam has been fighting for the rights of the Cherokee in Washington for years, and then he came here to attend the treaty signing at New Echota because Chief Ross had to stay in Washington. He tried to stop that travesty and on the way home was the victim of a brutal Indian attack that nearly killed him."

Iris was amazed at this interpretation of Adam Stuart's personality and goals. Had she judged him too harshly? All she'd seen was his surliness. But now his anger made a little more sense. It must have been hard for him to accept defeat. And then to be attacked by the people he was trying to protect...

⁊⦿

Adam wanted to get on his horse and race back to the other side of the river. Why had he thought a visit to the Indian village would help clear his mind? And why had his horse thrown a shoe just as he reached the turn to Brainerd Mission? He'd come to find the blacksmith and get his horse reshod so he could continue his journey. The fact that it was Sunday made no difference to him since he and God were no longer on speaking terms. He had planned to wait quietly outside until the services were done, get his horse tended to, and get on his way.

Pastor Miller continued lauding Adam's legal abilities, never realizing that his audience, Miss Iris Landon, was staring at Adam in shocked disbelief.

It was another indication of his bad luck to run into her after the scene he'd caused last week at her friend's house. What must they think of him? He didn't want to see the censure in Miss Landon's big brown eyes so he kicked a rock loose and watched it skip across the ground and disappear under the steps leading to the meetinghouse. What right did she have to judge him? She was new to the town, and from what he'd heard, she'd grown up in the lap of luxury in Nashville. She was probably just a slightly more rustic version of Sylvia—secure in her little world and her narrow beliefs. Well, he had news for both of them. They might think they knew it all, but that was because they'd never had to brave the world beyond their safe borders. He would like to show Iris Landon what the real world was like.

Righteous anger filled his heart. He would not allow these people to judge him. "Excuse me." The words came out in a low growl. Let them think what they may; he was going to escape. Adam turned on his heel and made his way into the meeting hall. Row after row of rough-hewn pews filled the main room. He supposed the preacher would stand on the raised dais up front so he could be seen by everyone.

Several of the pews were already occupied as Adam made his way to the front of the room and plopped down in the first pew. He'd show them that he was not afraid of them or their God. Condemning voices from the past filled his head as he sat there. They blocked out the rustle of a skirt as someone sat down next to him, but they could not compete with the wonderful fragrance that tickled his nose. Roses. Someone had brought roses into the room.

Adam looked to his right. Miss Iris Landon. Only she didn't look disgusted, angry, or even scared of him. She looked. . .concerned. Her wide brown eyes searched his face even as her smile made his jaw unclench. He wanted to return her smile. He wanted it more than he wanted to maintain his anger.

She was not Sylvia, after all. She was just as beautiful but in a more natural way. His gaze soaked up the details of the long eyelashes that fluttered downward modestly, her rosy cheeks, and the generous mouth that still hinted at a smile. His fingers itched to push back the curls escaping her coiffure. He reined in his traitorous thoughts. They were what had gotten him in trouble before, and he would not allow history to repeat itself.

Pastor Miller stepped up on the dais and opened his arms to the crowd. "I am pleased to see you this Easter morning. We Christians have so much to celebrate, especially on this day. Let's start the morning in song."

Adam listened to Iris's lilting soprano join in as the pastor sang "Jesus, Lover of My Soul." He let the words wash over him, bringing some comfort to his roiling thoughts. When the next song began, "Sun of My Soul," he allowed his own voice to join in. But his throat closed up when they reached the verse about a "wand'ring child" who spurns "the voice divine." His conscience roared to life, pushing him to his feet. Well, why not. He'd entered the service on a wave of anger. Wasn't it fitting that he exit on a river of remorse?

❧

Iris shifted to allow Adam past her. She wanted to reach out and touch him, but she kept her hand at her side. Instead she sent a heartfelt prayer to God to defeat the demons in his life.

She settled back against the pew and concentrated on Pastor Miller's message, but part of her mind worried about the tall man. Pastor Miller described Adam as a tireless defender of Indian rights. Perhaps she should give him the benefit of the doubt. It was a difficult time for anyone who cared about the future of the Cherokee. Perhaps if they'd met a year earlier, she would have seen another side of Adam. A charming, irresistible side.

When the service was over, she returned to the Millers' home and enjoyed a large dinner of ham, sweet potatoes, and early peas. She, Camie, and Mrs. Miller put the girls down for a nap before returning to the parlor to overhear Lance and his father-in-law discussing a visit to the Cherokee village at the top of Lookout Mountain.

"It's been a long, hard winter, and I'm worried that some of the villagers may be short on basic supplies," Pastor Miller explained. "You would be doing me a favor to go up tomorrow, and you could show Iris here the citadel of rocks."

Lance turned to his wife. "What do you think, dear?"

Camie looked apologetically at Iris before shaking her head. "I don't think it's a good idea to take the girls up there. It's still a bit too cold, and Emily started coughing as we were putting her in the crib."

Mrs. Miller came from the kitchen carrying cups, saucers, and a silver pot filled with aromatic coffee. Iris also recognized the spicy smell of fresh maple cookies. "Why don't you leave them here with us? It's the perfect opportunity to let Iris see a little of the country from up on high. And since your housekeeper is still away, I know you and Lance could use a break."

"I concur." Pastor Miller accepted a cup of coffee from his wife. "If Emily is getting sick, she probably ought to stay indoors for a day or two anyway."

Iris turned down the coffee but reached for a cookie. She passed the plate to her friend and bit into the treat, savoring the piquant flavor.

"You may be right." Camie's voice was hesitant. "Would you like to go, Iris?"

"Of course she wants to go." Lance answered before she could swallow the mouthful of cookie. "Don't you remember your first time on the mountain? Besides, I think your parents want a chance to spoil our daughters a little."

Iris thought a trip up the mountain sounded like a grand adventure if Camie was willing to go. She relished the idea of meeting with some of the local Cherokee, as well as seeing the view from the top of the mountain. The outline of the tall peak had intrigued her since her arrival.

Soon it was settled. Lance and Pastor Miller loaded the wagon with staples—coffee, flour, and sugar—to take with them while she described the changes in Nashville and the surrounding area to Mrs. Miller. Then the men came back in, and they all sat around discussing the mission's successes and failures in this part of Tennessee.

That night, as Iris pulled her quilt to her chin, she wondered what had happened to Adam Stuart. Then she wondered why she cared. There was something about the man, something that drew her to him. Was it her desire to share her faith with him? Or something else?

ten

"How far is the village from the mission?" Iris swayed with the wagon as Lance negotiated a sharp turn.

"About three hours by wagon," Camie answered. "We're almost there."

From the tall trees on one side of her, Iris heard the call of birds and the rustle of small animals. She looked toward the other side of the trail, surprised that she could only see the tip-tops of trees stirring at the touch of a gentle breeze. Dizziness attacked her vision as she tried to look down the slope of the mountain on that side, making her grip the slats of the wagon bench. "That's good."

Camie sat next to her husband on the front bench, but she must have heard the discomfort in Iris's voice. She turned around and laid a hand on her knee. "It's overwhelming at first. But wait until we get to the top. The view is awesome."

Lance guided the horses with care. "It always reminds me of how big God really is. He created so much, and we can only see the barest fraction of it."

Iris tried to make her smile less shaky for Camie's sake. She was determined to enjoy the trip.

The path opened up ahead of them, and suddenly she saw the village. The cluster of small mud-and-log houses reminded her of the Cherokee village close to Nashville. Women sat outside their homes cooking, sewing, or weaving on the looms donated by the government for their use. Several dogs ran to where they stood and barked vociferously, announcing their arrival to the tribe.

Camie waved and called out to a couple of the women as they made their way through the noisy animals. Soon they were in the middle of a laughing, hugging group. A few moments later the braves came out of the round council house, where they had apparently been holding a meeting.

Iris lost count of the names and faces as she was introduced around, but everyone was friendly and eager to learn about her. She told her story of coming to work for Mr. Spencer again and again, describing the children and their grandfather.

"If I didn't know better, I'd think you were following me."

The sardonic voice turned Iris's head. She forgot all about the Spencers. Her heart fluttered like a startled bird as her gaze locked with Adam Stuart's. "What are you doing here?"

"I could ask the same question. I thought you were visiting your friends at the mission."

Iris frowned. Was the man deliberately baiting her? His tone was certainly filled with sarcasm. Was that how he kept people at a distance? But why? Why would he be so eager to alienate her? He and Pastor Miller obviously admired each other. And even Lance seemed to have a grudging admiration for him. Maybe he had a problem with women. She remembered her prayer for God to help him. Was his presence here a gentle nudge from above to encourage her to befriend Adam?

"It's a pleasure to see you, too. I was hoping we'd have a chance to talk, but who would've thought it would happen so soon." Iris congratulated herself on her answer. From the surprised look on his face, her response had not been what he expected. "I wonder if you could show me around. Lance and Camie promised me an awesome view, but he's gone back to the wagon, and she's busy renewing old friendships."

Iris held her breath and watched the expressions crossing his face. Distrust, surprise, calculation, and finally surrender.

He offered his arm to her. "Why not?"

A little voice inside warned Iris that she had been too impetuous, but she would not back down now. She took his arm and grabbed her skirt in case his stride outpaced her own, but she need not have worried. Adam Stuart might be taller, but he was considerate enough to shorten his stride so she had no trouble keeping up with him.

"Where are you from?" she asked, eager to open a dialogue.

"I was raised in Virginia. My pa sent me to William and Mary. I earned a degree before going to Washington to open a business."

"My pa went to William and Mary, too, but he moved back to his parents' home in Nashville and married my ma. Did you like living in the capitol city?" She saw him glance her way, but she focused on the path before her.

"I guess it was okay. I met a lot of important people, people who are making decisions that will shape the future of our country."

"That must have been exciting. What made you come out here?"

The look in his eyes was dark and full of pain. What had happened? Had someone hurt him terribly?

He seemed to shake off the disturbing memories as he answered her. "Chief Ross asked me to set up shop out here and do what I can to help his people." He helped her slide through a narrow opening between two giant boulders that crowded against each other. "But enough about me. Tell me about your home. Why did your parents allow you to come alone to Daisy?"

Iris allowed him to change the subject, relating the reasons for her journey to Daisy, but she couldn't help wondering about the abrupt change. Something had happened to Adam in Washington, something to alter his outlook on life. If she could convince him to tell her about it, perhaps she could help him overcome it.

Excitement filled her as he led her onto a stone plateau that thrust itself out over the valley. She forgot his hidden problem as the world spread out before her.

❧

Adam saw the view as though he was looking at it for the first time, the way Iris must be seeing it. The citadel of rocks was an awesome place, perched at the very top of the mountain and overlooking the serpentine waters of the Tennessee River as it wound its way through the large, flat valley below. The sun had not set, but the moon had already risen in the east, its face turned pumpkin orange from the reflected blaze of the sun.

"Can you see the raft traveling toward Ross's Landing?" Adam stood close behind her and pointed to a small shape in the giant U of the river. He didn't realize anything was wrong until Iris slumped to the ground at his feet.

He knelt beside her, his heart climbing up into his throat. "Miss Landon? Iris, are you hurt?"

No answer. He lifted her gently against his chest and listened for her heartbeat. It seemed steady enough. In fact he couldn't find any reason for her to lose consciousness at all. He loosened her bonnet and pulled it off, checking to make sure there was no evidence of injury to her head. Nothing. Nothing but a profusion of curls that danced around her face. He was about to loosen her collar when Iris groaned.

Her eyes fluttered open. "What happened?"

Adam shook his head. "I don't know. One minute you were standing there looking, and the next thing I knew, you were swooning at my feet."

"I don't swoon." She glared up at him and tried to push him away, but Adam would not let go of her. He was relieved that she seemed to be recovering fairly quickly.

"Well, how do you explain it then?"

He could feel her shrug. "I think I got dizzy. The ground seemed to be moving, and then darkness swallowed me up."

"Vertigo." He nodded. "It's not a common complaint, but I have read of it." Now that he was certain Iris was neither ill nor wounded, he could relax and enjoy the feeling of holding her close to his heart. "It's caused by heights."

They sat like that for a few moments, as close as a breath. Her head was on his shoulder, her curls tickling his chin. He could have remained that way the rest of the day, breathing in the sweet scent of her cologne. But then she jerked. Was she having a seizure?

His alarm eased when he recognized the giggle that bubbled up from her throat. Iris put a hand over her mouth and glanced up at him, her eyes twinkling, inviting him to laugh with her.

Here he was thinking romantic thoughts about how perfectly she fit against his chest. He was a little offended that she found their situation humorous. Was she laughing at him? "What is it?"

She shook her head, loosening more curls in the process. Soon her hair would be tumbling around both of them. He could almost imagine how delicious it would look and the silky feel of it in his hands. His thoughts were disrupted by another giggle. This one ended in a hiccup.

Adam loosened his hold, and she sat up. "What is so funny?" he asked.

"I just don't understand how anyone so tall can have a fear of heights." Her eyes danced as she looked at him, inviting him to join the joke.

He chuckled. "Fear of heights."

She nodded and giggled again.

Adam couldn't help it. He laughed out loud. She laughed with him, the noise wrapping around him like a hug. The laughter built up inside him like a volcano, rushing to the surface again and again. He would think it was gone, and he would stop. But then he'd hear her still laughing, and it would overwhelm him again. He doubled over and laughed so long that he was sure his belly would be sore later.

He'd forgotten how good it felt to really laugh. There had been so little to even smile about over the past year. Life had become far too grim. But for this one evening he would forget about all his problems. Alone with Iris on top of the mountain, Adam determined that the rest of the world and its weary troubles could fade to insignificance.

Eventually their laughter abated. He stood and offered his hand to Iris, pleased when she accepted his help.

He glanced at her from time to time as they made their way back to the village. He was glad she had not put her bonnet back on.

As if she felt his gaze, Iris reached up and pushed the curls back from her face. "What I wouldn't give for a handful of hairpins."

Adam wanted to tell her how beautiful her hair was. How he thought it would be a shame to force it into submission. But those words would take them into dangerous territory. Territory he could ill afford to explore. He tightened his mouth and kept his attention on the path ahead, helping her when necessary and releasing her as quickly as possible.

Her friends fell on Iris the moment they entered the village. As Adam hung back, she glanced over her shoulder at him and smiled.

A butterfly tickled his stomach, an echo of their earlier merriment. It brought a smile to his lips, and he bowed to her as she disappeared into a group of eager Cherokee women.

❧

Iris wondered why God had seen fit to saddle her with such

impossible hair. It would not be tamed.

She let her bonnet hang down her back as she and Camie helped the Indian women prepare a meal. She peeled and chopped vegetables to go into a savory stew and then helped ladle the hot mixture into bowls and trenchers.

When everyone gathered to eat, she looked for Adam but could not see his familiar figure anywhere. She tried to tamp down the feeling of disappointment. Just because they had shared a few moments of closeness was no reason to expect him to stay around and keep her company. She sat down next to Lance and Camie and concentrated on her meal.

Lance sopped the last of his stew with a wedge of corn bread and patted his stomach. "We'd better head back so we can get down the mountain before it gets dark."

The local chief had some of the older children ready the wagon while Iris and Camie helped with the cleanup. Before long they were waving good-bye to their hosts and heading back down the mountain.

As Lance negotiated the steep path, Iris distracted herself from the dizzying views by wondering what had happened to Adam after they returned to the village. She felt like he'd shown her a side he rarely allowed others to see. The laughter they'd shared at the citadel of rocks was a memory she knew she would always cherish. It had been so good to see his anger and bitterness replaced by simple pleasure. Adam Stuart was a complicated man—intriguing, infuriating, and fascinating. Perhaps that was why she couldn't banish his handsome features from her memory.

eleven

Iris reached for her cloak and pulled it on. She was glad the past week had drifted by without alarms or problems. The girls had welcomed her back with warm hugs and soft kisses, and they had all settled into a routine as the outside temperature rose and the days began to lengthen. Every time she and the girls heard a horse canter up to the house, however, Iris rushed to the balcony to see if the visitor was riding a tall black stallion and sporting a creased suit. And every time, she turned away and tried to quell the disappointment that tightened her chest. She didn't know why she was drawn to Adam Stuart. There were several reasons she should want to avoid his company. But something made her want to help him.

She pushed aside thoughts of the intriguing Mr. Stuart as she prepared to depart. She had made plans to spend her afternoon off with Camie. They were going to town to shop.

"Why can't we go with you?" June asked, her hand bunched in the folds of Iris's cloak.

"We'll be very good." Anna stood on the other side, her face upturned.

Josephine walked into the nursery. "Now you leave Miss Iris alone. It's her afternoon off, and she needs to spend it the way she wants to."

"It's too far for you to walk, my dears." Iris knelt between them. "I am going to see my friend, Mrs. Sherer. You remember her, don't you?"

They nodded.

"We're going to do some shopping. If you are very good

and don't give Josephine any trouble, I'll bring each of you a peppermint stick."

Their faces brightened.

Josephine put an arm around each girl's shoulders. "I'm not sure they like peppermint."

As Iris descended the main staircase, she could hear June and Anna protesting that they loved peppermint more than anything else in the world.

Iris opened the front door and breathed deeply. Spring had finally come, and she was grateful. Warm sun kissed her cheeks as she walked along, considering what she would say if she saw Adam Stuart. Which facet would he show her the next time they met? Would he be the outlandish flirt, the angry pessimist, or would his hazel gaze and ready laughter remind her of the charming guide at Lookout Mountain?

Iris walked to Camie's house, her mood buoyed by her thoughts. The Sherers' housekeeper had returned from visiting her family in Georgia and was going to keep the twins while their mother shopped.

Camie filled Iris in on the latest news as she drove the wagon the two miles to Daisy. "Lance says that Nathan's uncle is on a rampage. He failed to get the council to go along with his latest scheme to take Mr. Spencer's farm away. He's apparently gone to the district judge to ask that the land be put up for auction."

"I cannot see how Nathan abides his uncle's attitude."

"You and I are more in the minority than you realize." Camie frowned at her. "A lot of people in Daisy don't think an Indian ought to have that nice a place."

"They're jealous of his success." Iris rolled her eyes. "Those same people are probably envious of your hardworking husband, nice home, and beautiful children."

"Jealousy and envy are strong emotions." Camie's lips straightened into a flat line. "It's why God warns us not to covet what our neighbor has."

Iris shook her head. "Well I, for one, refuse to worry about the malcontents in town. Mr. Spencer has owned that land for decades, and nothing is going to change that. Why, even President Jackson is not trying to remove Indians who own their land. The Spencers will be living in that house for generations to come."

Camie slowed the wagon as they made it to town. It was a good thing she did as a man came dashing out of Mr. Pierce's store and ran right in front of the wagon, his arms waving. "Remember the Alamo! Remember the Alamo!" He untied his horse from the hitching post, threw himself into the saddle, and galloped away.

"What do you suppose that was about?" Iris asked.

"I don't know, but why don't we go to the store and see what we can find out?" Camie climbed down and tied off the horse's reins.

From the sound of it, most of the town was there. The ladies had to push their way inside.

"Hi, Mrs. Sherer." The feminine voice belonged to a woman about their age. She was stunning, with exotic green eyes and shiny auburn hair.

Camie nodded at the beautiful woman. "Hello, Miss Coleridge."

The woman looked to Iris. "I don't believe we've met." She held out a hand, and Iris took it, instantly impressed by the indomitable spirit she saw in the woman's eyes. "Hi. My name's Margaret Coleridge. It's a pleasure to meet a friend of Camie's."

"Likewise." Iris squeezed her hand. "I look forward to getting to know you better."

"It's a small town." Miss Coleridge smiled warmly. "I'm sure we will bump into each other with regularity."

"What's going on in here?" Camie nodded toward the

crowd of people clustered around the long counter at the front of the store.

Margaret's expression grew serious. "It's bad news, I'm afraid. There was a battle in a place called the Alamo in Texas Territory. They are saying that Davy Crockett, our recent congressman, was killed in the battle."

Nathan sauntered over, wiping his hands on his apron. "It's worse than that."

Someone pushed past Iris, jostling her elbow. "What could be worse?"

"They're saying Davy and several others survived the battle and were assassinated after they surrendered."

Iris covered her mouth with her hand, her eyes filled with horror.

Someone banged on the counter with the butt of his gun. "Remember the Alamo!" The cry was picked up and repeated, making Iris feel uncomfortable.

Nathan nodded his head toward the door. "I think maybe you ladies should leave." He tried to guide all three of them to safety, but somehow Iris found herself carried in the other direction by the restive crowd. Even though she was tall enough to see over most of the men in the store, she could not push hard enough to get to the exit.

An elbow jabbed her in the ribs at the same time that a booted foot trod on her shoe, and Iris could feel herself falling. Panic clawed its way up her throat. If she fell here, she might be seriously hurt by the angry crowd.

A strong arm snaked around her waist, and Iris found herself with her nose pressed into a hard chest. "It's okay. I've got you." The man twisted so that he was between her and the shoving crowd then half-dragged, half-carried her to safety outside.

Iris pulled away from the strong arm, her mouth open to thank her rescuer. She looked up into blazing hazel eyes and snapped her mouth shut.

Adam Stuart pointed a finger at her. "You need a keeper, Miss Landon. Didn't your parents teach you not to go into a mob like that? Those men are ready to riot."

"Maybe so, but no one asked you to come to my rescue." Iris wondered what had happened to the appealing man at the citadel of rocks. Adam's charm had evaporated like early morning dew. She glared at him. "Why don't you mind your own business?"

Camie ran over to where they stood. "I was so worried." She hugged Iris close. "Thank you, Mr. Stuart. I would never have forgiven myself if anything had happened to Iris."

"Well then, maybe you should keep her on a shorter leash." He strode down the street without another word.

❧

Adam wanted to avoid Poe's Tavern, but tonight he had no choice. It was his job.

He had not been there since taking Iris—Miss Landon—on that tour up to the citadel of rocks. He didn't know what it was, but something about her purity and goodness made him want to be a better man. When he looked at the faith shining out of Iris's brown eyes, he had to wonder if God existed after all. And if He did, maybe the reason for the pain and death of this life was due to man's sinful nature rather than an uncaring Creator.

"Here you go, boy." He pulled a cube of sugar out of his pocket, fed it to his horse, and left the animal tied to the hitching post.

He entered the tavern, surprised to find it so crowded. It reminded him of the scene at Pierce's this morning. When he'd seen Iris foundering in the crowd, his heart had stopped beating. And then he'd scorched her with his words the moment he was sure she was safe. He would give his good leg to erase those angry words from existence.

A place had been made for him at the round table where the seven members of the town council sat. He shook hands with the ones on either side of him and waited for the meeting to begin.

Richard Pierce banged a miniature mallet against the table to get everyone's attention.

Adam pulled out his pencil, several loose sheets of paper, and the ledger he used for transcribing council minutes. From the sound of things, it was going to be a long night.

"Quiet! Quiet! I now call this meeting of the Daisy town council to order." Pierce waited for the noise to abate before giving Adam a regal nod. "Read the minutes from the last meeting, Mr. Stuart."

Adam opened his book and went down the list of items that had been discussed at the previous meeting. When he was done, he looked back at Pierce.

"Are there any objections to the minutes as read?" asked Pierce. The silence in the room was only broken by the tinkle of glass and the scrape of chair legs against the wooden floor of the tavern. "Then let the record reflect that the minutes were adopted without change." He banged his mallet again. "Now on to new business."

Someone coughed, and a low murmur began in the room.

Pierce raised the mallet once more and banged it loudly to regain their attention. "For the first order of the day, I think this council should consider a matter that causes me great concern. Now you all know that I'm a fair man." Someone in the back of the room laughed, but Pierce continued without pause. "I don't mind the Indians who live over there at Ross's Landing. I've even been known to sell them a few things just to keep the peace. But no matter what my personal thoughts are, I have to speak out about the danger that has sought refuge in our fair town."

Adam watched the man's face twist with hatred and distrust.

Why had God left such a man as Richard Pierce alive and well, while He took someone brave and honest like Davy Crockett away from them? This world needed more Crocketts and fewer Pierces.

One of the other council members stood up. "This had better not be about Wayha Spencer, Richard, because we've tabled that matter."

"Yeah, leave Spencer out of this." The voice came from a bearded man in the back of the room. "He's been here a lot longer than I have. Besides, we've got more serious matters to discuss, like what happened in Texas."

A general chorus of agreement stopped Pierce from continuing his argument. His face reddened, and he slumped back, crossing his arms over his chest.

For the next hour the men in the room suggested ways to support the Texans fighting for freedom from Mexican tyranny. Several men said they were leaving at daylight, while others pledged the support of ammunition and supplies. One of the council members proposed starting a list of men who wished to donate to the cause. His idea won support, and the meeting adjourned.

Adam gave them a sheet of paper and a pencil and then left them to figure out the rest. It wasn't part of his job to direct charitable efforts. He ambled past the men crowded around the table and sat down on his usual stool.

"Do you have any fresh coffee, Cyrus?"

The bartender nodded and walked away for a moment.

Before he returned, Nathan Pierce entered and took the stool next to him. He turned his back to the bar and faced Adam. "I know Crockett was a friend of yours, Adam. I'm sorry for your loss."

Adam hunched a shoulder and stared at the steaming mug Cyrus set in front of him.

"Are you going to Texas?"

"I thought about it." Adam indicated his bad leg. "What good is a limping solider? What about you?"

"No, my uncle needs me at the store." Nathan's cheeks darkened with a rush of blood. "And there's another reason I don't want to leave right now, a more recent development."

A ringing sensation filled Adam's ears, and his hands clenched. Icy fingers of despair wrapped themselves around his heart and squeezed. "Does this development have a name?" *Idiot,* a dark voice taunted him. *Did you think you were good enough for the likes of Iris Landon? Much better for Nathan to claim her. He'll take good care of her.*

Nathan's face reddened further. "Yes, but I'm sure it's not necessary. You must know which lady has caught my eye."

With a swift motion, Adam took a large gulp of the coffee, feeling the sting of the hot beverage on his throat. "My congratulations. Her heart is as big as the whole outdoors. She'll never play you false."

"There's only one problem." Nathan leaned closer to confide in Adam. "I'm not sure my uncle will approve of her."

Adam watched his hands tighten on the polished edge of the bar until his knuckles turned white. The man didn't deserve a woman like Iris if he was afraid she wasn't good enough for his pompous windbag of an uncle. "She may be a bit impetuous, but if your uncle is too stupid to recognize her qualities, then he doesn't deserve your consideration." Didn't Nathan Pierce realize how lucky he was?

A small voice whispered to Adam that he could not face this loss without help. And he knew the voice spoke the truth. For a brief instant he wished he had not severed his connection to God, but then he banished the thought and raised his hand to get the bartender's attention. He needed something stronger than coffee to cope with his pain.

twelve

"That cannot be allowed!" Iris tried to calm her voice, but it was the outside of enough. Lance Sherer had to be mistaken. "What does Mr. Pierce hope to accomplish by filing suit against Mr. Spencer?"

"I guess he wants to make sure Wayha goes west with the other Cherokee." Lance sighed. "And his position as mayor may lend him credence in a court of law."

Iris stood up and paced the floor. She glanced at Mr. Spencer, who sat at his desk saying nothing. Didn't he realize how serious the matter was? He could lose everything.

She turned to Lance. "But I thought you said the council and even some of the townspeople defended Mr. Spencer last night."

Lance nodded. "But it was what he said after the meeting that concerns me. He swore he would have Wayha's land no matter what. He said he was going to sue Wayha. If he files his complaint, it will be heard in the Superior Court of Law and Equity in Knoxville, not by a local judge who knows the real situation."

Mr. Spencer raised his head, and Iris could see the pain in his eyes. "Perhaps I should consider leaving after all."

"Don't even think about such a thing." Iris walked to the window and looked out. "You've built a wonderful life here, and no man has the right to take it from you." She turned to face him. "Didn't the Cherokee people own all of this land at one time?"

"No." Mr. Spencer shook his head. "We did not own the

116

land. It is the bounty of God. The Cherokee people have always lived here freely. It is only since the white man came that we have come to accept the idea of owning land."

"But this land does belong to you legally, doesn't it?" Iris asked.

A nod answered her question. Mr. Spencer looked at Lance. "You have my deed as proof."

Iris's feeling of relief died a quick death when she saw the expression on Lance's face. "What's wrong?"

"There's a problem with the deed."

Mr. Spencer's face turned as white as parchment. "What do you mean? There is nothing wrong with that deed. It was properly executed and signed."

"The problem is not with the deed. It's with the location of the deed." Lance's cheeks were ruddy with embarrassment.

"You have lost my deed?"

Lance shook his head. "I did not lose the deed. I. . . It was stolen from my house."

Iris gasped. "You were robbed? Is Camie okay? The children?"

His cheeks grew even darker. "I don't know when it happened. Someone broke into my office. He must have known the deed was there. We heard nothing. I'm not even sure when it happened, but he broke into my safe and rifled through all the papers."

"Who could have done such a thing?"

"I don't know." Lance turned to Mr. Spencer. "I will make this right. I remember reading that your land was given to you by the state of North Carolina as recompense for your service during the Revolution. I plan to draft a letter to the land grant office in Washington, asking for their help."

Iris had never considered how old Mr. Spencer was. But after hearing this news, he suddenly looked old enough to have fought with her grandfather in the Revolutionary War. This man deserved protection from greedy men like Mayor Pierce, and she would do everything in her power to make certain he was treated fairly. "Until you hear from Washington, we need to make sure Mr. Spencer's rights are protected. He will need to be defended by someone who is familiar with the court system."

Lance drummed his fingers on the arm of the settee as he considered their options. "It needs to be a man who is sympathetic to the Indians."

All three of them sat in silence for a few minutes.

Iris wished she could ask her pa for advice, but he wasn't here. Besides, she was an adult. She could come up with solutions on her own.

"There's only one man I know of who fits the bill." Lance tugged his collar. "Adam Stuart."

Iris frowned. "We can't ask him for help."

"Why not?" Mr. Spencer asked. "Adam is smart, and he'll know how to approach the case. He's our best chance."

❧

Iris sat next to Lance in the wagon as they made their way to town and Adam Stuart's office. "I don't think this is a good idea."

"I know, but who else could we ask? Besides, Mr. Spencer trusts him."

"So does Pastor Miller." Iris wished she trusted Adam. At first she had taken him to be a libertine because of his behavior on the night she'd arrived in town. But he'd disproved that assessment when he'd taken her to the top of Lookout Mountain. He'd been the perfect gentleman, even though she had swooned in his arms. And she couldn't fault his concern for the Cherokee. If only he could shake off the cloud of bitterness surrounding him, she was sure he'd be an outstanding citizen and the perfect advocate for Mr. Spencer.

"Lance, who do you think could have taken the deed?"

His face tightened. "I have no idea. Few people knew it was there. You, Camie, Wayha. . ."

He left off the last name, but she heard it in her mind. Adam. Again she questioned whether or not they should turn to him for help. Yet who else was there? Adam knew more about Indian rights than any other man around. She prayed for God's guidance and felt peace settle around her like a cloak.

Adam Stuart was an intriguing man—full of contradictions. No one else had ever had the power to rouse her anger so quickly. She considered his rescue yesterday. She had to admit she had been frightened when she was separated from Camie and unable to make her way out of the crowd. But after he got her outside, his attitude had been inexcusable. And he had run off before she could express her thanks or much else. Today would be different. Now that she'd had time to fully recover her equilibrium, she would not let him annoy her again.

Lance pulled up on the reins and climbed down from the wagon. Normally Iris would have scrambled down without any help, but several curious people were watching so she waited until he tied the horses to a post and came around to assist her in disembarking. She felt the gazes of the townspeople on them as she followed Lance to the door.

Lance knocked, but no one answered. "I hope he's here." He tried the doorknob. "It's not locked."

Lance pushed the door open and waited for Iris to precede him.

"Hello," she called out. "Is anyone here?"

The office was dusty and dingy. Not at all what she had pictured for an attorney. Of course, this attorney probably worried very little about things like simple housekeeping chores.

A thump and a groan from the far side of the room answered her query. "Who's there?"

Lance shut the door behind them. "It's Iris Landon and Lance Sherer. We're here to hire your services."

A series of thumps and bumps sounded, and then a hand came up from the far side of Mr. Stuart's desk and rested atop it, followed by a second hand. They pressed against the surface of the desk. Then Iris saw a head of light brown hair that made her think of coffee with cream, followed by the pale, haggard face of Adam Stuart, attorney at law. He bore more resemblance to the scarecrow Grandpa Taylor used in his cornfield than a professional lawyer. His coat was missing, and his hair looked like it could use a thorough brushing to remove tangles, twigs, and dust. His shirt was unbuttoned and hung slightly open, exposing an indecent amount of his chest.

"This is ridiculous." Iris could feel her cheeks burning as she turned to Lance. The peace she'd felt earlier melted away. "There must be someone else who can help."

"Why don't you step out to the wagon for a moment, Iris. I'll see that he gets cleaned up."

Iris couldn't look toward Adam again. She held her chin up to mask her embarrassment on behalf of the pitiable man and swept out of the office.

The sun moved slowly toward the west as she waited. They were making a terrible mistake. Mr. Spencer would be better served if they sent for someone from Nashville or even Knoxville. Surely there were competent attorneys who could also manage to stay sober.

Finally Lance came out to collect her. "He's better now." He let her in and went back to Adam's living area behind the office.

The scent of coffee was strong in the room. Iris hoped it would have a salutary effect on the man they'd come to see. The man who might very well be Wayha Spencer's only hope.

❧

Adam's head throbbed, and his mouth felt like it had been stuffed with cotton. He wanted to slink back to his bedroom and sleep for a few days until the embarrassment wore off, but he forced himself to walk back into the office and face her. How could he have fallen asleep on the floor behind his desk? And why did Iris have to pick that particular day to visit his office?

Nathan Pierce would never have found himself in a similar situation. Which was why Nathan Pierce deserved her, and he did not.

Adam peered at the vision as Iris moved farther into the office. Did she have to be so beautiful? She was as tall as a statue and twice as lovely. A statue, however, could never capture the warmth and caring that shone from her eyes.

He dropped his gaze. It must be the alcohol still swimming around in his head that was making him so crazy. He had to get her out of here. "I can't help you."

He heard her shock in the swift intake of her breath. "You don't even know what I need from you."

He pasted a smile on his face. He'd had ample opportunity to mask his true feelings. "Lance explained about Spencer's trouble with the law. Some men would say I should not aid a slave owner."

"Let's address one problem at a time, Mr. Stuart." Her voice was strained, and he could see desperation in her eyes.

Her pain tempted him to change his mind, but Adam refused to be drawn into a battle that had already been lost. "I told Wayha weeks ago to clear out, and he wouldn't listen."

"So that's it." She huffed. "You won't even try to help us?"

Adam shook his head.

"I had planned to tell you that I was sorry for thinking you were no more than a bitter man who wanted to live in the past. It is not my right to judge you, but as a Christian I can deplore your actions and decry your cowardice."

How dare she pass judgment on him? Hadn't she said it was not her right? "I suppose it was a coward who rescued you from certain harm yesterday, too?"

That stopped her.

"You're right, of course. You did protect me, and I owe you my thanks."

"What? No more denunciations?" He stepped from behind his desk and walked toward her. She didn't shrink back like most women would have done. She squared her shoulders and glared at him through those disdainful brown eyes. He wanted to shake some sense into her. She should go back home to Nashville before she found herself on the wrong end of a lynch mob for defending an Indian. This country of his was not going to see reason when it came to the Cherokee, and the sooner everyone agreed, the better it would be.

"No, although you sorely try my patience." She took a deep breath. "I will not let anger control my words or my actions."

Adam couldn't have been more surprised if she had produced a pail of water and dashed him with it. How could she decide to not get angry? And yet he could see the calmness that entered her eyes. If he reached out for it, he could have almost caught the ire that rolled away from her, leaving her serene and peaceful.

"How did you do that?"

She looked confused by his question. "Do what?"

"How did you get rid of it? It's not like you tamped it down. I could sense it leaving you as though it were an uninvited guest."

"I get my strength from the Lord." She smiled at him, the sweetness plain to see. " 'Cease from anger, and forsake wrath: fret not thyself in any wise to do evil.'"

"I know the verse." Although it had been a long time since Adam had read his Bible, he was familiar enough with David's psalms to recognize the words. "That chapter promises that evildoers will be cut down as easily as grass, yet evil still flourishes."

"That's because of the devil's wickedness here in the world of men. It will not always be so." She leaned toward him.

Adam was the one who backed up a pace when he caught a whiff of her perfume. It was too heady a mixture for his poor head. "Then we may as well give up and get along until God decides to come back and straighten us out. He doesn't seem to be in much of a hurry."

"Don't you see, that's because of you and me. It's up to us to spread the Gospel. God is long-suffering and wants everyone to be saved. I believe it's the reason He is allowing the white man to overrun this land."

"Because He likes white men better than Indians?"

Iris shook her head. "Because we are bringing His message with us. At least some of us are."

He ignored what might have been a jab at him and attempted to ignore the inner jab that he knew came from Someone else. "So how does that fit with greedy land grabbers? And what about Davy Crockett and the others who died at the Alamo? How does that fit into God's plan?"

Adam was shocked to see unshed tears in Iris's expressive eyes. Was she sad for Crockett? Spencer? Him? He didn't have the nerve to ask.

Lance came back into the room bearing a dented coffeepot and several mugs, one of which was so cracked Adam doubted it would hold liquid. He was embarrassed all over again for Iris to see the conditions in which he lived.

He looked around at the dust and dishevelment surrounding them. It had been so long since he'd cared about the niceties of life. Lately he'd been more interested in getting through each day. Perhaps it was time for him to rejoin the living.

He could almost hear the call to arms. It was the same call that had filled him once before with the need to defend Indian rights. Suddenly he was tired of all the pretense. It was time to stop hiding from the future. Hope filled his chest and made his heart beat faster. He straightened his shoulders and smoothed the wrinkled material of his suit coat. Adam had almost forgotten how exhilarating it could be to strive for fairness and justice.

This case against Wayha Spencer was nothing but a trumped-up accusation. Who knew? He might even enjoy routing the pompous mayor in the courtroom. "Tell me about the deed."

thirteen

The past week had been tense as Iris waited for Adam to report on the progress of Mr. Spencer's case. This afternoon she was determined to distract the girls by teaching them a new game. She surveyed the pattern she'd drawn on the dusty ground with some satisfaction. Her ma had taught her the game of scotch-hoppers when she was a young girl. The layout she had drawn was fairly small to accommodate June's and Anna's shorter legs.

She handed a rock to each girl. "Now, what you do is toss your rock into the first square right here." She dropped her own rock to show them and waited while each girl followed her action before gathering up her skirts. "The object is to hop into each square except the one that holds our rocks, but the trick is to use only one leg."

Iris demonstrated by hopping up through the ladder of squares she'd drawn in the grassless area behind the Spencer home. "When you get to the round space here, you can rest on both feet for a moment before returning to the start."

The girls clamored for a chance to try their luck, so Iris sent June first and then Anna. When each girl had returned, she had them pick up their rocks and toss them into the second square.

The sound of someone clearing his throat nearby made Iris spin around and drop her skirts with a gasp as she recognized Nathan Pierce's broad shoulders and handsome face.

"Oh my!" Iris wondered if she would survive the embarrassment of knowing he'd seen her acting like a hoyden with her skirts around her knees. She lifted her chin in defiance. What did she care? She was doing her job, after all. "I thought it would be a good idea to give the children something energetic to do this afternoon."

He smiled and nodded. "I understand."

"Were you looking for Mr. Spencer?" she asked.

"No, I wanted to talk to you about a matter that causes me some concern." He glanced toward the girls, who were noisily arguing over whether June's foot had landed inside one of the squares. "Is there somewhere we can go?"

Iris clapped her hands. "Girls, please go to the kitchen and ask Cook if she can prepare some refreshment for our guest." She raised a hand at their protests. "If you don't go now, we won't be able to finish our game before it gets dark."

The girls looked at each other, and she could almost see the thoughts churning through their active minds before they ran back to the house, calling out to the cook.

Nathan's sigh of relief reminded her of his aversion to children, and she wondered if it was because he had no siblings. She couldn't imagine growing up without her own sister and brother. A wave of homesickness hit her as she thought of them.

"Thank you so much, Miss Landon." Nathan stepped close and took her hand in his own. "I thought it prudent to come and warn you."

Iris forgot about home as she concentrated on the man in front of her. "Whatever is the matter?"

"Everyone in town is talking about the amount of time you've been spending with Adam Stuart."

She pulled her hand free. He'd come to warn her about gossip? She shook her head. He must know that his uncle had brought a suit against her employer. Did he expect her to do nothing? "Yes, I have hired Mr. Stuart to defend against your uncle's complaint that Mr. Spencer and his family should be removed from their land."

"I know, and I hope you will understand when I say I do not support my uncle's actions. But I don't think it's necessary for you to hire someone to defend the Spencers. I cannot believe any judge would rule against them."

"That might be true if his deed had not been stolen from Lance's home."

Nathan frowned at her. "When did this occur?"

"No one knows, but it must have been taken by someone who intended to harm Mr. Spencer since it's the only document missing."

Nathan spun around and paced toward a stand of trees, obviously considering the information she had given him. She thought of the night he and his uncle had come to dinner at the Sherers' home. Could Mayor Pierce be the culprit? He was the most obvious suspect to her because he was so determined to have the Spencers removed. She watched as Nathan turned around and retraced his steps to stand next to her.

"I know you must blame my uncle, but I cannot believe he would stoop to thievery." His earnest face beseeched her to agree. "He's an honorable man."

Sympathy filled her. Nathan was being more reasonable than she would have been in his place. And perhaps his uncle was innocent. At this point it didn't much matter what had happened to the deed. They simply had to find other evidence to prove Wayha's claim was legitimate.

Nathan took her hand in his. "You will not want to hear this, but there is a more likely candidate. The very man you hired. He has been quite vocal in his opinion that the Spencers should give up and move west before it's too late."

Iris blew out a disgusted breath. "Adam Stuart would never do such a thing."

"I believe you are right. He would not do anything dishonorable. . .as long as he was sober." He squeezed her hand. "The night he came to the Sherers' home, he was anything but."

She shook her head. "I won't believe it."

Nathan shrugged and let her hand go. "You should at least consider it before you condemn my uncle. I know he can be a bit overbearing, but he is a good man. Uncle Richard is much more likely to fight honorably than resort to underhanded means." He left her alone then, his words echoing in her mind.

Iris hated to admit it, but there was some truth to what Nathan said. Alcohol often stripped away the morals of honorable men.

Could Adam have taken the deed that night? Was she being foolish in trusting him to defend the Spencers? Yet he seemed so intent on working with her to keep the Spencers in their home. Was it all a facade? No. She shook her head. It could not have been Adam. He might not be perfect, but Adam Stuart was not a thief. . .she hoped.

fourteen

Adam could feel anticipation welling up as he turned onto Wayha Spencer's land. He couldn't wait to see the beautiful, courageous Iris Landon. When she had turned to him for help two weeks ago, she'd turned his whole world around. He would do everything in his power to see that Wayha kept his land.

Earlier this morning he'd gone to visit Lance Sherer about the missing deed. The paper had not turned up, so everyone had to assume it had been stolen. But who had taken it? Who could have known that it was being stored there? When Lance had first suggested that he keep it, Adam had been certain it was the perfect solution. If Iris's God did exist, He certainly did work in mysterious ways.

Adam had been about to return to town, but then he decided to ride out to Wayha's home. He tried to tell himself it was a logical way to gather more information to help the case, but deep inside, he knew he was hoping to see Iris. What was it about her that drew him? He was like a callow youth who had fallen in love for the first time. He could not get enough of her beauty and spirit.

He dismounted and handed his horse's reins to the slave who met him at the front entrance. Josephine greeted Adam, but before she could lead him to Wayha's study, he heard the clatter of feet hurrying down the staircase.

He looked up to see the granddaughters. Although they were of different ages, they looked very much alike with their dark hair and shiny brown eyes. When they spotted him, they stopped their headlong progress and looked back up the stairs.

His gaze followed theirs, and he found himself drinking in Iris's beautiful visage. No wonder her parents had named her after a flower. There was something so clean and bright and sparkling about her. She looked like a fresh blossom, especially in the lavender dress she was wearing.

She descended the stairs gracefully. "It's a pleasure to see you, Mr. Stuart."

"Likewise," he answered, wishing he could think of something intelligent to say. What was it about Iris Landon that tied his tongue in knots? "Are you taking these young ladies outside?"

Iris reminded them of their manners with a glance. "June, Anna, you remember Mr. Stuart. He's working for your grandfather."

The older girl curtsied, followed by her little sister.

He bowed. "My, how grown-up you've become. I'm sure your grandfather is proud to have such lovely young ladies about the house."

"Miss Iris, can he come with us?" June asked.

Iris shook her head. "I'm sure Mr. Stuart is here on business. We must let him meet—"

A door opened, and Mr. Spencer came into the hallway. "I thought I heard voices."

"Yes sir," Iris answered the older man. "The girls and I are going on a picnic down by the stream. We'll leave you and Mr. Stuart to your business."

Wayha shook his head. "I have matters to attend to in Ross's Landing." He turned to Adam. "I'm sorry you came all this way, and I can't stay."

June tugged on Adam's pant leg. "That means you can come with us."

Adam smiled down at her. "There's nothing I'd like better."

He glanced toward Iris. "If I wouldn't be in the way, that is."

Anna, not to be outdone by her sibling, moved closer to him. "We have lots of food. And Miss Iris is going to show us how to catch fish."

He noticed a heightened flush in Iris's cheeks. Was it caused by anger or excitement? He hoped it was the latter. He was certainly anticipating an enjoyable afternoon.

The house slave handed a basket to Iris, but he took it from her. "The least I can do is carry the food since you have been so kind as to invite me along."

Iris tied shawls on the girls and straightened her hat before they headed outside. Adam offered her his arm, pleased when she rested her hand on it. They ambled slowly down the path that led to the stream behind the house. She didn't seem to mind his uneven gait, a fact he was thankful for.

"Be careful. Don't get too far away," she called out, ad-monishing the girls who had skipped ahead of them.

"Are they always this excited?"

Iris nodded. "They have a natural ability to enjoy the simplest of things. It's such a pity that their mother and grandmother died. They are starved for affection." She blushed slightly and looked away. "Not that Mr. Spencer doesn't love them. He's just. . .just reserved."

"My father was much the same." Adam looked ahead to the sparkling blue waters of the deep stream. "But I never doubted his love for me."

"I thought we could spread our blanket near that tree." Iris pointed to a tall maple. "That way we can get out of the sun if it grows too hot this afternoon."

Adam set the basket down and took the blanket from atop it, spreading it out on the ground and anchoring it on all four corners with rocks. At the same time, he picked up several smaller flat rocks and dropped them in his coat pocket.

When he was done, he joined the girls, who were exploring the banks of the stream.

"Did you see that?" June pointed to a ripple in the water. "It's a fish."

Anna pointed, too. Her eyes grew round as a dark shape broke the surface once more. She jumped up and down on the sloped bank, and Adam reached to grab her before she could fall into the swiftly flowing water.

"Be careful. Miss Iris would be very upset if she had to jump in the water to save you."

Anna looked back toward the tree where Iris was setting out food for their lunch. "Miss Iris can do anything."

Adam laughed at the faith in the little girl's voice. "I'm sure she can. But let's not try swimming this afternoon. Would you like to learn how to throw rocks and make them jump across the water?"

Both girls nodded, so Adam pulled his stones out. He gave one to each child and chose another for himself. He bent down and showed them how to hold a rock between the thumb and forefinger. Then he tossed his out across the surface of the stream where it bounced one, two, three times before sinking below the water.

June bent her arm back and threw her rock with all her strength, but it only plopped into the water. When Anna tried for the first time, her rock did not quite reach the water's edge.

Adam pulled more of his rocks from his pocket, and the three of them tried again and again. After a little while Iris wandered down to where they stood. He could feel her gaze on them and turned to catch her smiling.

"Come here and show us how well you can do it."

&

Iris couldn't help but compare Adam's ability to entertain and charm her girls with Nathan's discomfort the day he'd come to see her. Of course Nathan had his own charm and many excellent qualities, but it was Adam who was winning June's and Anna's hearts.

She clapped her hands as Anna managed to get her rock into the water. "What talented girls you are."

"Did you see me?" asked June. "My rock bounced two times."

Anna ran to her. "Can you bounce a rock, Miss Iris?"

"Oh, I doubt it."

"Come on. Mr. Stuart can show you how. He showed me." June added her own endorsement. "And me, too."

"Here." Adam handed her a rock. "This is a good one. I'm sure it will bounce several times."

Iris took the rock and turned it over in her hand. She had no idea how to throw the thing to make it skip. Skipping rocks was something she and Camie had never tried. She tossed the small stone toward the water, twisting her arm to add extra power. The silly thing didn't bounce a single time.

"Try again." Adam's voice was encouraging as he handed her another one.

"I don't know. We don't want to fill the stream with all these rocks."

Adam's laughter made her smile. "I don't think there's any danger of that." He moved directly behind her. "Here let me show you how to do it."

Iris's heart jumped up to her throat as she felt his arm encircling her. Her back and shoulders stiffened, but he didn't seem to notice as he took her hand and turned it sideways.

"Hold the rock loosely." His breath tickled her ear, and his nearness reminded her of the day he'd shown her the citadel of rocks.

She'd been breathless that day, too.

Iris tried to concentrate on the method he was trying to

teach her. She let him manipulate her wrist back and forth. Then he snapped her hand forward. The rock flew out of her grasp and sailed out over the water. Her eyes widened as she saw it skip again and again before falling below the surface.

"I did it!" She twisted around in her excitement and came face-to-face with him. Their lips were only inches apart. If he puckered slightly, he would be kissing her. Everything seemed to slow down. As if from a distance, she could hear June and Anna congratulating her. But all she could see was Adam's face. Some shred of sanity made her pull away from him, but it took several seconds before she could breathe normally. Apparently she was no more immune to his charm than June and Anna.

Iris herded the girls back to the blanket, relieved that their chatter covered her embarrassment. She sat down and took several deep breaths in an attempt to calm her still-racing heart. Why did it beat so hard against her chest when Adam was present? And why wouldn't it even flutter when she was around Nathan?

২৯

Adam took a deep breath to steady his racing heart. He'd been so close to kissing Iris. Right out here in the open and in front of her charges. What had he been thinking? If she had not pulled away, he would have yielded to the temptation. While he was thankful her reputation was still intact, a part of him longed to pull Iris back into his arms and never let her go.

He stood alone on the bank of the small stream and watched as she settled the children on the blanket and handed each of them a piece of chicken. Maybe he should leave them alone. Just then, Anna looked toward him and waved her arm.

"Come and eat, Mr. Adam."

He walked to where they sat, wondering what he could say

to reassure Iris. "Perhaps I should return to town."

June's eyes rounded. "But you'll miss the best part if you leave now."

"That's right." Anna nodded solemnly. "Miss Iris promised to tell us a story."

He tried to read Iris's expression, but she had her face turned away.

"Well, perhaps I can stay for a little while." Adam sat down on the blanket. "Is Miss Iris a good storyteller?"

"The best." June looked toward Iris. "What story are you going to tell us?"

"Tell the one about the lost sheep," Anna suggested. "I like that story."

Iris placed a piece of chicken on a plate and handed it to Adam. "But you already know that story."

Anna's bottom lip protruded. "Please, Miss Iris."

"Well, if you're certain." Both girls nodded at her, so Iris took a deep breath. "Once upon a time, a young shepherd boy loved his sheep very much. . . ."

Adam munched on his chicken as Iris began to talk. This should be interesting. He was familiar with the story, but it had never held much meaning. What kind of shepherd would leave his flock to find one lost sheep? Better to protect the ones left in his flock.

Yet as Iris talked about the shepherd's concern, he felt a tug on his heart. Then she described the shepherd's joy, and he felt it, too. The excitement of finding something that was lost. The celebration of not only the shepherd but also the other sheep, as they welcomed the lost lamb back to the fold.

He was so lost in contemplation that Adam didn't realize Iris had finished the story until he felt a small hand tug on his shirtsleeve. He looked down into June's earnest face.

"Don't you like that story?"

Adam cleared his throat. "Yes. It was a wonderful story." His voice sounded gruff even to his own ears. He glanced at Iris. Could she tell how much her story had affected him? Somehow she had brought the scripture alive this afternoon. No wonder it was the children's favorite story. It was well on the way to becoming his favorite, too. Of course it was only that. A sweet story. It would be nice if the real world worked that way. But he knew all too well that it didn't.

How wonderful it would be to feel so loved, so prized. But Adam's mind balked at the idea of God trying to return him to the fold. Not when he'd been so eager to blame God for all his problems. Not when he'd strayed so far from the path. He didn't deserve that kind of love, and he knew it.

fifteen

The next few weeks passed in a whirl of activities. Adam rode over to Dallas, a community some miles to the north where they had a telegraph office. He sent queries out to the nation's capital as well as to Raleigh, the capital of North Carolina, where records of land grants were recorded and should be housed. The documents he was trying to find out about, however, were neither listed by location nor by owner, making his task harder.

Iris came to town to visit him at least twice each week, and they would spend hours poring over faded land grants, old deeds, and ambiguous records. He would always regret not kissing her that day by the stream. She'd been so close. If only the Spencer children had not been there, he might at least have dropped a peck on her cheek.

Since then he'd been careful to keep a discreet distance between them. He didn't want to scare her into avoiding him altogether. At first she had been stiff and wary of him, but that had eventually worn off as they worked side by side toward the same goal. She usually brought something for them to eat, and Adam made certain nonchipped crockery and clean surfaces were available for their shared meal.

The two of them created a list of dates and facts substantiated by the documents still in Lance's possession and the reports they received from Adam's queries. He would have liked to have the original deed in hand, but since it had disappeared so mysteriously from Lance's home, he suspected it would never again surface.

The court date was only a week away. It was time to pack up the evidence and say good-bye to Iris. He rolled up the last map and tamped it into a tube to take with him to the courtroom. "I will be back in less than two weeks."

"I don't know why I cannot come with you." Iris frowned at him over her plate of yams and sliced ham.

"Yes you do. Wayha will have to go with me so he can testify on his own behalf. He trusts you to watch over his grandchildren while he is away."

She rolled her eyes. "I know, but still I want to be there."

"I know you do. I'd like it, too. But you know you cannot go." He put a hand over hers and squeezed it gently.

She allowed her hand to stay there for a moment before pulling back. "Maybe Camie could stay with them."

"No, Iris." He sat down across from her. "It's far better for you to stay here. We have a strong case. Please trust me to see that Wayha's rights are protected."

"I do trust you, Adam. Why would you do all this work and not defend him well in court?" She smiled at him. "No matter the outcome, I'll always be grateful for the effort you've put forth on his behalf."

Adam wished he had the right to lean across the table and kiss her. She had such faith in him and his ability to save her employer. He only hoped it was well placed. If he won, maybe he would tell her how he felt. He could tell her how much he admired her spirit and her positive outlook. He could tell her how he wanted to bury his face in her hair and drink in the delicate aroma of her perfume. He would explain how she'd brought him back to life and given him a reason to continue, a reason to stay away from alcohol. He'd not been tempted to go to the bar once, even when he had to attend council meetings at the tavern.

"I hope you know how special you are, Iris."

She blushed at his words. "Dozens of women are more special than I am. You should talk to my great-aunt Dolly. She'll tell you that I have never been a proper female. Parties, fancy dresses, and exchanging recipes hold no interest for me."

"Believe me, the women who are interested in such things are not worthy of consideration."

Her expression became serious as it often did if she was concerned about something or someone. It was another of the qualities he admired in her. "Adam, I think we've grown to know each other fairly well over the past weeks."

He nodded.

"May I ask why you are so cynical about women?"

It was his turn to blush. He could feel the hot blood rushing to his cheeks. He didn't want to think about what had happened in Washington, much less explain it to Iris. But if he ever hoped to have a future with her, he had to be honest with her about his past. He took a deep breath and released it slowly. "There was a girl who I thought loved me, but it turned out she loved her comforts more."

"I'm so sorry. Did she break your heart?"

He nodded, choosing his words carefully. "Sylvia was the beautiful, sheltered daughter of a powerful attorney in Washington. And I was a radical newcomer with lots of lofty ideas. It wasn't her fault. I swept her off her feet. For a little while, everything was okay. I thought she needed time to understand how reprehensible it was to remove the Indians from their land." Adam stopped when he felt Iris's soft hand cover his for a moment. The gesture warmed him and gave him the strength to continue. "But she thought I would give up on Indian rights, take a job in her father's firm, and escort her to all the right political galas."

"She expected you to give up your principles?"

"She thought her world would appeal to me. And when it

didn't, she looked around for another candidate. Someone her daddy would approve of." Adam still remembered the shock of finding that his best friend and business partner was going to take his place as Sylvia's fiancé. But the memory had lost its sting. He looked into her eyes, hoping Iris could see the love he now felt for her. "I once thought I'd never love again, but it turns out that a heart can mend."

Her eyes widened, and she leaned away from him.

Her reaction made him clamp his mouth shut. She was not ready for him to declare his love. Maybe she never would be. That's when he realized that a mended heart could shatter again.

sixteen

Adam was glad to be back in familiar territory. His heart pounded with anticipation as he knocked on Wayha Spencer's front door. He had missed Daisy while he was away. Or rather he had missed one of Daisy's inhabitants, namely Iris Landon. Although Wayha would have told Iris the outcome yesterday when he got home, Adam wanted to celebrate their victory with her.

He was let in by the house slave and shown to an empty parlor. As he waited for Iris to appear, he thought about the last time he'd come here and the thrill of holding Iris in his arms as he showed her how to skip rocks. And then the time they'd spent together in his office. Nathan might be a better prospect as a husband, but no one else knew Iris the way Adam did.

In a way, he could hardly believe it had been two weeks since he'd left Iris to go to court. The time had been very busy—more than a week traveling and four days in court arguing Wayha's position. It had taken all his legal skills and Wayha's sincerity to convince the judge, but it had been worth their efforts. He paced from one end of the parlor to the other, eager to tell Iris how the evidence they had collected together had convinced the judge that taking Wayha's land would be a terrible mistake. Wayha and his granddaughters were safe.

The door opened. She stood, a vision in her pale lavender gown. He let himself savor the moment. An expectant, hopeful look filled her beautiful face. Her glorious hair was escaping from the restraint of pins and ribbons as always and framed her face.

He was drawn closer to her as a moth to an irresistible flame. "Iris, you are more beautiful than the flowers you are named after."

A becoming shade of red flagged her cheeks, and she smiled at him. "So we were victorious?"

He nodded and took three long strides across the room to stand next to her. Taking hold of her hands, he leaned back and started to spin, causing her to swing around and around until they were both breathless and laughing. Her eyes were luminous with joy, and a wide smile showed her even teeth. She looked just the way he'd imagined.

He described the twists and turns of the trial, how grasping Mayor Pierce had appeared on the stand and how well Wayha had answered every question asked by the plaintiff's attorney.

"I wish I'd been there," said Iris. "I would have loved to see you in the courtroom."

Adam had dropped her hands while talking about the trial, but now he took them in his again. "Maybe we can do something about that." He drew her a few inches closer.

Her laughter disappeared instantly. "Wh–what do you mean?" Her breathy voice, so near his ear, sent his heart soaring. She seemed as affected by their nearness as he was.

"Will you do me the honor of becoming my wife?" He knew the words were a mistake the minute they were out of his mouth. Where was the eloquence that had helped him win in the courtroom? He'd meant to start by telling her how much he admired her. She was the kindest, most endearing woman he'd ever met. Her honesty was like a breath of fresh air blowing away the doubt and betrayal of his past.

Iris's whole body stiffened, and she pushed against his chest.

Adam wanted to hold on to her long enough to say the words that crowded in his mind, but he didn't want to frighten her. So he let her go. She sprang away from him with all the force of a ricocheting bullet. In an instant she had moved to the far side of the room, strategically putting the settee between them.

"I'm not any good at this, Iris. I want you to know—"

"Please stop, Mr. Stuart."

He noticed that she had gone back to using his last name. Not a good sign. He closed his eyes, his mind going back to another beautiful woman who had broken bad news to him. Was she going to break his heart as Sylvia had done? This time he wasn't sure if he would recover.

"I blame myself for this situation. I probably led you on by allowing informality to creep into our relationship because of the hours we spent together before the trial." She stopped talking for a moment and looked toward the empty fireplace.

"You could never lead me on, Iris." He intentionally used her first name. Maybe her hesitance was an indication that she did love him. Maybe if he could prove his case to her, she would judge him worthy. "I have changed so much because of you. Look at me. I'm sober and ready to fight once again for the rights of the Cherokee to keep their lands. I have even been thinking about moving back to Washington so I can once again work with John Ross and the other Cherokee leaders to overturn the treaty signed at New Echota. My home and my whole life are clean and orderly because of your influence."

Her gaze turned back to him, and Adam could see the sadness. She opened her mouth to answer, but he knew he had lost before she uttered the first word.

"Adam. . .Mr. Stuart, while I am flattered and touched by your declaration, I cannot accept your kind offer." Her voice broke a little on the last word. She cleared her throat before continuing. "The things you mentioned are important, but I cannot link my life to a man who has not allowed God to clean him up on the inside."

Her words stung like an angry wasp. Could she not see how much he had changed? Why did she have to ask for his total commitment? God hadn't argued Mr. Spencer's case or obtained a favorable ruling. Adam had. It was the logical outcome of their hard work and intelligence, not some benevolent figure protecting the innocent.

Adam hardened his heart to keep it from breaking beyond all hope. "I am sorry you don't think me worthy. I'll take my leave now." He dropped the deed to the Spencer holdings on a convenient table. "Please see that Mr. Spencer gets that."

"Wait, Ad—"

It was the last thing he heard as he slammed the parlor door on her. Would he never learn how quickly a woman could send him from the heights of joy to the depths of despair?

seventeen

Iris walked into Richard Pierce's store with her head held high. She wasn't sure how Nathan would react to his uncle's loss in court. They'd all nodded to each other at church last Sunday, but the two men had disappeared soon after the services were over.

She lifted her chin as she passed through the front door. A quick glance told her Nathan was working at the counter. She wandered to the fabric section of the store, fingering several bolts as she tried to decide what would be suitable for making new dresses for the girls and herself.

"I've been saving a special bolt of material in the back, in case you came by, Miss Landon." Nathan's voice tickled her ear.

Iris jumped slightly in surprise. She turned, breathing a sigh of relief when she saw his welcoming expression. Tension she had not even realized she harbored drained away from her shoulders. "That's very sweet of you, Mr. Pierce. I would love to see it."

He smiled, showing his even, white teeth. "I'll bring it right out."

She browsed through the rest of the material as she waited for his return, wondering why Nathan did not make her heart stutter or beat faster in spite of the fact that he had startled her earlier. It wasn't fair. He was a good man. A good *Christian* man.

She'd only had to pass Adam Stuart's shuttered office to set her traitorous heart thumping. He was the opposite of all the things she held dear. She would simply have to get over her feelings for him. Why had she ignored the danger until it was too late?

She thought back to the day Nathan had come to warn her about working with Adam. A sardonic smile curled her lips. She should have listened to him and avoided putting her heart at risk.

Iris had been certain she was immune to romantic notions. No Nashville suitor had ever roused the least interest. But then, no man in Nashville had Adam's zeal for justice. No one else had invited her past his crusty exterior to see the warm, vulnerable heart underneath.

"Here it is." Nathan proudly held a bolt of lavender cotton for her inspection.

"It's perfect." Iris didn't have to feign appreciation. "How thoughtful of you to realize my favorite color and hold it for me."

"I'd like to do even more for you." He glanced toward the counter and then back at her.

She looked into earnest blue eyes that had picked up some of the color of the material he held against his chest. Perhaps she could fall in love with Nathan if she tried a little harder. "I think your uncle might have something to say about that. He knows how I feel about Wayha's rights. And he is bound to be upset about the judge's verdict."

He frowned. "Uncle Richard has forgotten all about that, and I hope you will, too. Especially now that Congress has ratified the New Echota Treaty. He says it is only a matter of time until everything works out."

Iris felt her heart drop to her toes. So the treaty had been ratified. A major step toward removal, it was a blow in the fight for Indian rights. Maybe Adam knew what to do next. But that was silly. Hadn't she just been thinking about distancing herself from the dangerous Adam Stuart?

She allowed Nathan to lead her back to the counter and waited while he wrapped her material in a piece of heavy paper. His smile made Nathan look even more handsome. Maybe she did feel a flutter. A tiny one, anyway.

She was trying to decide how to answer him when the front door flew open and banged against the wall. She looked up to see the recent subject of her thoughts marching toward her, his limp more pronounced than usual. He was furious. She didn't think he'd been this angry the day he'd saved her from being trampled by the riot.

"I hope you're happy now." He slapped a newspaper on the counter in front of her.

She looked down and read the headline: TREATY RATIFIED BY SINGLE VOTE. "Nathan told me. It's a shame, but—"

"A shame? I suppose you could call it a shame." Adam's voice shook. "And the worst part of it is, I almost fell for your loving God. When the judge ruled with Mr. Spencer, I began to hope He would protect the Cherokee and stop the United States government from stealing Indian land. But I was obviously wrong. What kind of God would allow this to happen?"

A couple of ladies who'd come in to purchase sundries were staring at her and Adam. Iris wanted to sink through the floor. She could not believe Adam had chosen to air his feelings now.

Apparently Nathan agreed with her. He stepped from behind the counter and took Adam by the elbow. "This is neither the time nor the place, sir. You are disturbing my customers, and I would like for you to leave. If you must air your complaints, I will come by your office later this afternoon and we can talk."

Adam shook off his hand. "I've had my say."

Iris watched as he stalked across the room, looking neither to the right nor the left. The door slammed behind him.

Ignoring Nathan and the other shoppers, Iris perused the article. President Jackson must know the treaty was a sham. John Ross, the elected chief of the Cherokee, had not even been present when it was signed. According to the reporter, Ross had been vocal in his condemnation of the treaty, as well as of the men who had signed the document. Yet Congress had chosen to ignore his protests. "This is so sad."

"Why do you say that?" Nathan asked. "No one forced the Cherokee to sell their land."

She folded the paper and laid it back on the counter. "The whole thing is disgraceful. Apparently, a small group of men signed the treaty without the agreement of the Indian leaders. They didn't even represent a majority of the Cherokee."

"I heard there's gold on some of that land." He shrugged and returned to the far side of the counter to pick up her bolt of material. "The Indians don't want it for themselves, but they don't want to let anyone come in and mine it. Why shouldn't they accept a fair price and move away?"

Iris stared at Nathan. She could feel her blood heating at his cavalier attitude. Had he not thought about the situation? "What if they don't want to move away? What if they love their land in the same way that Mr. Spencer does? What if they want to pass their heritage down to their children and their grandchildren?"

"I guess they can do that when they relocate." He continued tying the twine on her package as though the matter under discussion was unimportant. When he finished, he patted her hand kindly. "They'll be free to follow their own way of life without interference from white men."

Iris didn't know if he meant to sound as patronizing as he did. Perhaps he didn't realize how condescending his smile was. As though she was too simple to understand the issues involved. She wanted to ask if he agreed with his uncle's trying to take her employer's home, but she didn't have the nerve. What if Nathan confirmed her suspicions?

She suddenly felt like she had more in common with Adam than she would ever have with Nathan.

❧

The council meeting was over, and Adam was ready to go home. He wondered why he was still here in Daisy. He ought to be in Washington fighting for the Cherokee with every legal argument he could dream up. Last month's victory for Wayha Spencer had reawakened his thirst for justice.

He didn't need to worry about Sylvia Sumner, who had probably married his erstwhile partner by now. He hoped she and Jeremy were happy.

Happier than he was.

Night after night, he relived the last time he'd seen Iris. With Nathan. He supposed Nathan had overcome his reluctance to tell his uncle about his feelings for Iris. Good. Iris deserved someone nice to take care of her. Not a bitter cripple.

Pain in his hands made Adam look downward, surprised to see his fingers gripping the table so hard his knuckles had turned white. With a conscious effort, he relaxed his chest, his shoulders, his arms, and finally his fingers. Then he stood and headed toward the door, horribly aware of his unsteady gait. He passed the bar without waving good-bye. At least he didn't feel the urge to sit back down and have a drink.

Adam made his way to his office and kicked open the door with his good leg. It was dark and empty, a homecoming he should get used to. Why expect more? Wasn't life full of harsh realities and broken dreams? His life certainly was. Every time it seemed things might be turning around, something happened. Like the ratification of the New Echota Treaty...

And having to watch the courtship of Nathan Pierce and Iris Landon.

eighteen

The delicious aromas of roast pork and gravy rose from the table as Anna's childish voice blessed their luncheon.

After Iris had filled each girl's plate with food, she concentrated on her own meal. A few small bites and she dropped her fork. It was odd that she had so little appetite these days. She wasn't sleeping very well either. Ever since the day Adam had confronted her about the treaty ratification. As if it was her fault his world had crashed once again. She knew she wasn't responsible, so why did she feel guilty? Or was it something else she felt? Something like heartbreak?

"Can we go outside this afternoon?" June asked around a bite of meat.

Iris's concentration returned to the girls. She owed them her full attention, so she shook her head and dabbed at her lips with a snowy white cloth napkin before speaking. "A lady should not talk with her mouth full."

June made a show of swallowing her food. "I'm sorry, Miss Iris. May we go outside this afternoon? The sun is shining, and Josephine said there is a nice breeze."

Iris glanced at one of the windows. "Perhaps we could take a stroll after our meal. I would like to pay a visit to Camie since her parents are staying with them this week, and I know how much you two enjoy playing with her twins."

Anna whooped her delight but subsided when Iris frowned at her. "As much as we would all enjoy an outing, perhaps we should stay here and practice our deportment instead."

The two girls concentrated on minding their manners for

the rest of the meal, quietly finishing their food.

Iris hid a smile. Her charges could be a handful, but they were fully capable of ladylike behavior for the right incentive, much like she and her siblings had been.

When they had completed their meal, Iris told Josephine their plans and helped the girls with their bonnets. They skipped through the door and onto the porch while Iris followed more sedately. The three of them walked briskly down the lane and reached the main road that led to town, admiring the bright colors of wildflowers dotting the landscape.

"May we pick some flowers?" asked June. "We could take a bouquet to Mrs. Sherer."

Iris nodded. "I think that's a wonderful idea."

June and Anna ran ahead of her and began gathering blossoms. Iris strolled along more circumspectly, enjoying the bright sunshine and the laughter of the girls. She soon had an armful of blossoms. "That's probably enough for today."

"Look, I found an iris!" Anna ran up with a purple flower in her hand.

"It's not an iris." June's voice was strident. "Tell her, Miss Iris. Anna thinks she knows everything."

"I don't, either."

June stuck out her tongue at her younger sister.

Iris was about to admonish the pair when she heard a wagon coming down the lane toward them.

Anna held a hand over her eyes. "Who is that?"

"I don't know." Iris wasn't concerned. They weren't far from the Sherers' farm. It was probably Lance or Camie. She watched as the wagon trundled around a curve, preceded by a man on horseback. Her heart thumped when she realized they had pulled lengths of cloth over their mouths and noses. They couldn't be worried about chapped faces at this time of the year.

"Come here, girls." The flowers were forgotten as she pulled June and Anna onto the side of the road, her arms gathering them close. She began to pray for protection. There was no way to outrun the men, even though every part of her screamed that they should try to reach the distant woods.

The horseman rushed past them on the road, but when Iris began to hope that the men had some distant goal, he pulled up and brought his mount dancing back toward the three of them. The wagon came to a stop directly in front of them.

They were effectively blocked from fleeing. Iris took a step back, drawing the girls with her. Her eyes widened when the driver of the wagon pulled a rifle from under his seat and leveled it at her heart.

☙

Adam encouraged his horse to a canter as he turned down the road toward the Spencer estate. John Ross had sent him a petition and asked him to gather signatures from Cherokee who opposed the New Echota Treaty. Wayha Spencer was a good place to start.

Adam promised himself that he would maintain his distance if he saw a certain curly haired charmer. Iris might stir him in ways no other woman had, but she had made her feelings clear. She was too good for the likes of him.

His thoughts were interrupted by the sound of a galloping horse in the lane behind him. Adam twisted in his saddle, a groan escaping him as he recognized the wide shoulders of Nathan Pierce. From the looks of the fine suit he wore, the man was coming to see Iris. A sardonic smile twisted Adam's mouth. Iris's God must be intent on torturing him. He nodded to the man.

Nathan pulled up his horse as he reached Adam. "Where are you headed?"

"Same as you, I imagine."

The other man's cheeks flushed. "I. . .thought maybe. . .I wanted. . ."

Adam clucked his tongue to get his horse moving again. "You don't have to tell me what you plan. I can guess your intent."

Whatever the man would have answered was lost as Wayha Spencer's carriage rushed around the curve in the lane behind them. At first Adam thought the horses were out of control, but then he realized the driver was whipping the team to increase their speed. Wayha himself was driving them. He rushed past them without a pause, heading for the house at breakneck speed. Some calamity must have occurred.

"Come on!" Adam slapped his horse's reins and leaned forward, intent on finding out what had happened. His heart was in his throat.

Please let Iris be all right. The words formed in his mind and became a chant as he rushed to the house.

He swung down from the saddle and waited impatiently for Nathan to dismount. Together they hurried into the house through the front door, which stood open.

Wayha, his clothing liberally spattered with mud, was shouting at his slaves and servants. "Where are they? Have you looked everywhere?"

Josephine stood in one corner of the hall, among a group of hand-wringing women. The three menservants were shaking their heads, their faces showing varying degrees of dismay or concern.

"We must find them right away!" Wayha's voice was strident. He turned to Adam and Nathan. "Do you have news of my granddaughters?"

Adam shook his head. "No. What's happened?"

"They've disappeared."

Nathan stepped in front of Adam. "Where is Miss Landon?"

Wayha frowned. His normally placid face showed deep lines of concern. "With them, I hope. They should have been back an hour ago. They didn't show up for dinner. Miss Landon told Josephine they would be back."

"Where did they go?" Adam could feel dread tightening his chest.

"To the Sherers' home. Her father and mother have come from Brainerd Mission to visit."

"Have you gone to look for them there?" Adam asked the obvious question.

"Yes. They never arrived."

Nathan frowned. "How long have they been gone?"

Wayha looked different—old and scared. In all the time Adam had known him, he'd never seen the man show fear, not even when it looked like he might lose his home. But then, his grandchildren had never been in physical danger before.

Adam led the man to a chair and helped him sit down. "It's going to be okay, Wayha. We'll find them."

It took several minutes, but he and Nathan rounded up Wayha's menservants and slaves and sent them in different directions to scour the countryside. They were to knock at all doors and ask after the missing girls and their nanny then meet back at Wayha's home later in the day.

Adam went toward town, beating the bushes and checking every grove of trees. He couldn't find any evidence of Iris or the children. As the sun dropped lower in the sky, he headed back to the Spencer home, hoping one of the other men had been more fortunate.

His hopes were dashed as he was met by Wayha before he could even dismount.

"Have you found them?"

Adam shook his head, his heart heavy in his chest. "There's

no sign of them anywhere."

Nathan was only a few steps behind Wayha. "Where can they be?"

Adam accepted a cup of water from Josephine but refused to dismount. He was determined to keep looking. There had to be somewhere else for him to search. He had a feeling he was overlooking something.

Hooves sounded behind him, and Adam turned to see who was coming. It was a lone horseman. Lance Sherer, unless he missed his guess. Maybe the man had good news.

One glance at his grim face destroyed that notion.

Lance drew his horse up next to Adam's and dismounted. "I have nothing to report."

"I've been thinking." Nathan's hesitant voice seemed to come to Adam from a distance, nearly drowned out by a ringing noise in his head. "I may have an idea about what's happened."

Adam tried to lock out the emotions roiling in his chest. He didn't have the luxury of yielding to despair. "What do you mean?"

Nathan's gaze focused on the floor. "Earlier this morning, my uncle fixed up a big order for a couple of drifters who came into town last week. I never saw them pay anything for all the food and staples, which is odd enough. Uncle Richard has never been the type to encourage charity. And he told them to disappear for a few days."

Lance's voice was dismissive. "So your uncle gave away some food. Maybe he needed some work done on your house or the store and paid the men in supplies."

Nathan looked up. His eyes narrowed as he seemed to consider the suggestion. Then he shook his head. "No. The man said something about a concealed valley—"

"I found something." The last of Spencer's slaves ran toward them carrying a wilted bunch of wildflowers that he handed to Wayha.

Adam could hear Josephine's moan of despair, but he ignored it as he turned to Nathan. "You think your uncle took those children?"

Nathan's cheeks reddened, but he nodded. "It makes sense. Uncle Richard was so angry about losing to Mr. Spencer in court. But then his ire just went away. I thought it was because of the treaty, but what if he was planning something more immediate?" He glanced toward Spencer. "He may demand a ransom."

Spencer shook his head. "Whatever he wants, I will give if he will release my granddaughters. But where could he have taken them?"

"Have we tried all the empty houses?" Adam searched each of their faces. "Maybe Nathan's wrong. Maybe they were scared by someone and sought sanctuary in one of the abandoned cabins hereabouts."

"But where?" Nathan asked the question, but Adam saw it reflected on all the other men's faces.

That was the real question. There were dozens of places where they could be hidden. Since the massacre at the Alamo, several homesteads had been left vacant as outraged men headed south to fight the Mexicans. Places like the cabin where he'd recovered after the attack last winter. . .

The idea burst on him like a lightning bolt. The cabin was situated deep down in a ravine, a concealed valley. It was far enough away from town to avoid detection but close enough to contact allies if needed. "I think I know where they might be."

The other men swung to look at him. "Nathan, you and Lance go get the sheriff. I'll take Wayha and find the girls, but we may need help to get them out safely."

"Let Wayha and Lance get the law. I'm going with you.

If my uncle is involved in this, you'll need me to talk some sense into him."

Adam considered his words for a moment before nodding. He turned to Wayha. "I'll need some paper and a pen to draw a map."

They followed the Cherokee inside.

When Wayha produced the requested items, Adam drew a rough map for them to give to the sheriff. He hoped it was clear enough for them to find his destination. "Bring the men as quickly as you can."

The sun was setting as he and Nathan remounted their horses and took off toward the cabin. Every mile seemed to take a century as Adam's imagination kept supplying pictures of Iris cringing in fear from her captors.

He found himself praying, turning to the God Iris worshipped. The God he had once worshipped. Was He really there? Did He care about the tribulations of those who cried out to Him? Would He listen to someone who'd turned away from Him?

The questions twisted round and round in his mind, while the steady hoofbeats echoed in his head in time with his desperate pleas. *Keep her safe, Lord. Please keep her safe.*

nineteen

Mayor Pierce lit a candle and set it carefully on the small table in the center of the cabin. For a minute Iris thought they'd been rescued, but then she saw him handing money to one of the men who had abducted them and realized he had paid for the kidnapping to be done. He gestured to the other man, and both of the mercenaries headed outside, for guard duty she guessed.

The light flickered wildly, showing Iris the frightened faces of the Spencer children, who had been bound to chairs on their arrival several hours earlier. She tried to communicate reassurance and hope with her glance, but she doubted she was overly successful as she was also securely tied to a chair.

Iris tried to loosen the ropes around her hands as she watched the pompous man pace the floor of the small cabin. At least the children had a chance to get away from this unharmed. She knew Wayha would turn over the deed—or do anything else for that matter—to secure their safety.

Whether or not she would escape was something else entirely. Pierce seemed to blame her for the situation, and he had to know she would testify against him if she got the chance. No, there was no way he was going to let her go. A tremor shook her shoulders.

Pierce must have seen the movement. "I'm sorry for your discomfort, but it's necessary. Spencer will be ready to see reason when he finds that I hold something he values even more than his land."

Anna and June. A wave of revulsion swept through her.

What kind of man threatened children? Her gag prevented Iris from expressing her disdain. She glared at the mayor.

"Wayha never should have had that land anyway. No Cherokee should be given a legal deed. Trying to act like white men." He pointed a finger at her. "I thought I took care of that when I took the original deed from your friend's house."

Her shock must have shown on her face because he chuckled.

"Yes. I knew it had to be there. I know how to read people. I saw the look that passed between Sherer and his wife the night we all had dinner with them. I burned the deed and waited for my chance to take over that pretender's claim. But then you had to stick your nose in the business."

The mayor's expression sent a cold shiver down her back. He would never release her alive. It was obvious from the way he glared at her.

She closed her eyes to pray for the girls' safety and the strength to face whatever was coming.

❧

It took longer than Adam had hoped for them to reach the valley and plan the rescue. But at least it looked like they had found the right location.

What little was left of the sun's rays could not find its way into the ravine. As Adam crouched in the shadows, a part of his mind pleaded with God to keep Iris and the Spencer girls safe. All his doubts and questions were swept away in a tide of desperation. What if they had already been hurt. . .or killed? He pushed the thought to the back of his mind. He had to believe God led him to this place so he could save Iris.

Twigs popped and branches rustled as the man guarding the west side of the cabin approached Adam. Another guard was patrolling the east side, but Nathan would take care of him.

Closer and closer the man came, until it was finally time

to act. In one swift movement Adam pounced, overpowering the stranger with ease. Adam used a length of rope he'd brought to tie the man's hands and feet. As soon as he was certain the guard was secure, Adam crept forward as quietly as he could, listening for Nathan's signal.

The hoot of an owl alerted him.

He cupped his mouth and returned the signal. Then he took a deep breath and rushed the front door, shoving it open with enough force that it bounced against the wall and swung back toward him. He dropped to one knee. His gaze swept the room.

❧

Iris fought against her restraints at this new threat. Then the flickering light shone on the man's face, and hope sprang anew in her chest. Her prayers had surely been answered. "Thank You, Lord." She mumbled the words into her gag as she recognized the man who'd come for them. It was Adam!

Gone was the cynical, rumpled attorney. In his place was a crusading warrior. He surged forward and slammed into Mayor Pierce. Down they went, turning over and over as each man sought to gain control of the other. They exchanged punches, but it was clear Adam was much stronger.

"Stand down."

Iris had been so engrossed in the battle she failed to realize another man had come inside. Nathan. But was he here to rescue them or to help his uncle?

Her eyes widened as he drew his gun, and she tried to break free of her bonds once more. A moan of pain rose up as the harsh rope abraded her wrists.

"It's over, Uncle Richard."

It took a moment for his words to penetrate, but then Nathan's uncle stopped fighting. He glared at his nephew as Adam tied his hands together.

Nathan came to her. "Are you all right?"

Iris nodded. She could feel his knife sawing through the ropes that held her hands together behind the chair in which she sat. Ignoring the pain as blood rushed back into her hands, she pulled off the dirty cloth that had gagged her for the past hours. She rushed to the girls and gently removed their gags while Nathan freed them from their bindings.

Horses snorted outside, and then the little cabin was filled with people. The sheriff took control of Mayor Pierce and the drifters who had brought them to the cabin earlier. Wayha entered the cabin in a rush and hugged his granddaughters close, joy apparent on his face.

"I'm so sorry, Iris." Nathan's face was drawn into a deep frown. "I had no idea."

She patted his hand. "How did you find us?"

"It was Adam. He realized that you might be here."

"Thank God." Iris looked toward Adam, but he would not meet her gaze. She wanted to go to him, but if she did, would she be giving him false hope? The attraction was strong in spite of the insurmountable obstacles between them. Perhaps she should concentrate on comforting Nathan who was feeling the weight of his uncle's guilt.

❧

Adam could feel her gaze on him, but he kept his attention on Wayha and his grandchildren. If he looked at Iris, he was sure he would be unable to resist taking her in his arms and declaring his love for her once more. He could not bear the thought of embarrassing either of them again. Nathan was eminently capable of comforting her. Adam slipped outside to make sure the sheriff didn't need any help.

A little while later Nathan brought Iris out of the cabin. She seemed unharmed but subdued as Nathan led her to his horse and helped her into the saddle.

As though from a distance, Adam watched Nathan mount up behind her and wrap a protective arm around her waist. She never looked toward him. And why should she? She had Nathan taking care of her. Adam watched as they rode out of the valley together, taking a piece of his heart with them.

Wayha Spencer was the next to come out of the cabin. He had an arm around each of his grandchildren. Tears filled his eyes as he made his way to Adam and thanked him for reuniting them once more. The joy on the older man's face eased Adam's pain and brought a smile to his lips. Was this the same joy that Christ had described on finding the lost sheep? Was this how God felt when one of His children was returned to Him?

The thought nearly brought him to his knees. Adam pushed back the emotion in his throat. He nodded to the Spencer family and limped to his horse. An overwhelming desire to talk to someone about his revelations had him mounting up and heading to the Sherer household, the image of Reverend Miller's welcoming smile vivid in his memory.

&

Adam slid from the saddle and tethered his horse, relieved to see light in several of the home's windows. He was glad they were not abed. He would have hated to awaken them to talk to Reverend Miller, but the fire in his soul would not allow him to wait until morning. He rapped on the front door and tapped his foot as he waited for someone to answer.

Camie Sherer opened the door. "What is the news? Are Iris and the children safe?"

Adam reassured her and her parents, explaining that Lance had accompanied the sheriff to town and would be arriving shortly.

By the time the explanations were done, Lance had arrived, his face quizzical. "Is there something else wrong, Adam?"

"No. . .not exactly. I. . .I have something to talk to Reverend Miller about. Something that can't wait."

Lance nodded and drew his wife and mother-in-law out of the room. "We'll be praying for you."

Silence permeated the room. Adam wondered where to start. "I've done so many terrible things."

Reverend Miller regarded him somberly and nodded. "So have we all."

"I. . .I thought God was against me. I blamed Him for my troubles."

"Son, God loves you more than you can imagine. He made you. He knows you, and He's anxious for you to turn your life over to Him."

Adam felt a huge pressure in his chest as his emotions threatened to overcome him. He didn't deserve such love or forgiveness. "I want that forgiveness and love more than anything, Reverend."

Reverend Miller put a hand on his shoulder. "And God wants to forgive you. All you have to do is ask."

"But how can I? I've always blamed Him for my problems."

"There's always a temptation to blame the Creator when things go wrong. Are you familiar with the book of Job?"

Adam considered. The glimmer of hope that had appeared back at the cabin became a beacon, a warm, guiding light that was leading him home. "I think I understand. Job clung to God even though he lost everything."

"Exactly." The older man smiled at him. "We have much to learn from Job's reaction when God answered his complaints." He opened his well-worn Bible and turned to the final chapter of Job. " 'I have heard of thee by the hearing of the ear: but now mine eye seeth thee. Wherefore I abhor myself, and repent in dust and ashes.' "

"Yes, that's exactly the way I feel." Adam was relieved to

know Reverend Miller understood what he'd been trying to explain. He felt like a curtain had been drawn back, revealing the true nature of everything. He'd been so foolish, so blind, so arrogant.

"Would you like to pray with me?" Reverend Miller got down on his knees and folded his hands in front of him.

Feeling a bit self-conscious, Adam followed his example. He closed his eyes and listened as the preacher began speaking to God as though He was a personal friend. He thanked God for bringing Adam back into the fold, for loving them all, and for sending His Son to make salvation possible.

Lord, please forgive me for blaming You and for my many sins. Thank You. I know I don't deserve Your love, but thank You. And. . .thank You for not giving up on this lost sheep. The words signified the beginning of a new relationship, one that Adam knew would make his life worth living.

twenty

Iris entered the parlor and smiled at her visitor. Nathan was such a nice man. He had been stoic in the face of his uncle's trial and conviction for kidnapping. Not that anyone blamed him. Camie had told Iris that Nathan was being considered to take his uncle's place on the town council. The community of Daisy would benefit from having such an honest, upright man serving it.

Nathan swept her a bow. "It's a pleasure to see you, Miss Landon."

"Likewise. I trust you are well." She sat down on the sofa. "How are things at the store?"

Instead of sitting down, Nathan paced the floor. He walked to the window, looked outside, then turned and came back to where she sat. He rubbed a hand against one leg of his trousers and swallowed hard. Then he knelt in front of her. "I don't want to talk about the store, Miss Landon. . . Iris. I have a more pressing matter to broach." He took her left hand in his.

Iris's heart seemed to stutter for a second before resuming its steady pace. This was her second proposal of marriage. Where was the breathlessness she'd experienced when Adam proposed? She looked into Nathan's hopeful eyes and was overcome by a feeling of sadness. She knew how she had to answer this kind man. She was flattered by his attention, but she did not love him.

"You are a beautiful and intelligent woman, and I hope you will agree to become my wife. I know you must have seen how much I care for you. I will provide you with all the luxuries I can afford."

Iris tugged her hand free. "Please stop, Nathan."

His blue gaze searched her face. "Is it because of my uncle?"

"Of course not." She took a deep breath. "You're a wonderful man, Nathan, and you're going to make some lucky lady very happy one day—" She stopped. "Please get up, Nathan. I can't talk to you like this."

He rose and settled on the straight-backed chair next to the sofa. "I don't understand. I have the store, you know. I can afford to take care of you."

"That's not it, Nathan. One of these days, you're going to meet someone special. Someone who fires your imagination and makes your heart beat faster just because she's in the same room with you, breathing the same air."

He nodded slowly. "Is that how Adam makes you feel?"

Iris could feel the blush filling her cheeks. Was she that transparent? She'd seen Adam several times in town, but he'd never looked in her direction. This, however, was not the time to be thinking about Adam. She concentrated on the man sitting next to her. "Nathan, you're a wonderful man, and you deserve a wonderful wife. Someone who loves you. While I esteem you and appreciate all your many kindnesses, I don't love you in that way."

He glanced at her, the hope in his gaze slowly giving way to acceptance.

"But I hope we can still be friends." She gave his hand a friendly pat.

Nathan sighed. "Of course we will continue to be friends. You're a warmhearted woman. Perhaps I can eventually change your mind about us."

He was such a nice man. But what she'd told him was true. He deserved someone else, someone who would cherish each day with him, fall asleep with his name on her lips, and wake up thinking of him. Not someone who couldn't get another man's face out of her head.

వ

Adam opened his Bible and read once more about Paul's experience on the road to Damascus when he was still Saul. Like Paul, he'd been certain he knew all the answers—he'd been full of self-righteousness. But that changed the afternoon Iris was taken. He was forced to face the truth. His fear had blinded him, but when the scales fell away, he saw the truth. God was the One in control. And no matter whether Adam understood why things happened the way they did, he now believed that God would work it all out in the best way possible.

He placed the Bible on his desk and glanced at the petition lying next to it. There had been a steady stream of men coming from Ross's Landing and beyond, as word spread about the effort to stop the government from executing the New Echota Treaty. He already had more than five hundred signatures.

He looked up as the door opened. His practiced smile slipped. "Iris, what are you doing here?" He put a hand to his forehead. Where had that come from?

She drew herself up straight. "I'm sorry for disturbing you." She stepped back and started to leave.

He got up to halt her retreat. "No, Ir. . .Miss Landon, please don't go. I didn't mean to be so rude." It didn't matter why she'd come, only that she was near.

She turned back toward him, bringing a breath of freshness with her.

He caught a whiff of perfume that made him think of blooming flowers in the meadow back home. Why did she have to be so beautiful? He ached to pull her into his arms.

But she belonged to a better man than he would ever be.

She wandered past him to the desk where they'd spent so much time poring over dusty law books together and ran a finger over its surface. "I...we...the girls and I...have missed you. Have you... How have you been doing?"

Was Iris nervous? The thought made him want to comfort her. But that was Nathan's job not his. "I've rediscovered a thirst for justice. Once God got His message through my thick skull, I realized how wrong I was. How could I give up when He didn't give up on me? So I've been using my legal expertise to help other Indians like you and I helped Wayha."

"Adam, that's wonderful!" Her voice lost its hesitancy. Her eyes were wide and shiny with unshed tears.

Emotion clogged his throat. He'd better change the subject before he broke down in front of her. "I've been meaning to call on you to check on Wayha and the girls. But it's been so busy. I have to save as many as I can before the removal is enforced. And then there are all the settlers moving here to explore for gold. . . ."

What was he saying? She already knew about all that. "I'm sure Nathan—" He stopped on the word. This was harder than he'd imagined it would be. He took a deep breath and asked God for strength. "I'm sure your fiancé has been keeping you informed about everything."

Her eyes opened wide. "What did you say?"

"I—" His throat seemed terribly dry. He swallowed hard and opened his mouth once again. "I haven't seen you since your engagement."

"I beg your pardon?"

Why was she looking at him like that? Like he was not making sense. "You and Nathan will make a wonderful couple." He forced the words out. It wasn't like he hadn't practiced them. Every day for the past few weeks, as a matter of fact.

"I. . .best wishes on your upcoming marriage."

Her hat slipped to one side.

Adam's fingers ached to straighten it.

"I'm afraid you are mistaken, Mr. Stuart. I am not contemplating marriage with Mr. Pierce. He's not the man I'm in love with."

It was Adam's turn to stare. Hope bloomed in his chest like flowers in springtime. He pulled out a chair for her. Her perfume wafted past him once again as she sat down in the chair—the chair she had used while they worked together to protect her employer's rights. She leaned back and looked up at him. The tears in her large brown eyes had been replaced by a sparkle.

Adam pulled a chair into alignment with the one she occupied and sat down near enough that their knees almost touched. She did not demur or back away, which kicked up his heartbeat another notch. "I asked you a question a few months back."

"Yes?"

He cleared his throat. Pressed his knee up to hers. "But now the question is a little different due to the wonderful change in my life. Would you consider marrying a Christian attorney?"

"Oh Adam. . ."

Her voice was so low that Adam feared the worst. She was going to break his heart again. He stood up and turned his back on her, concentrating on his breathing. He was going to survive this. God was with him.

And then he felt her touch on his shoulder. He turned.

"Adam, I would like nothing better than working with a certain Christian attorney in his mission to save the Indians from injustice."

He drew a deep breath. "You mean. . .?"

She smiled at him. "Yes, Adam. I'll marry you."

His breath left him in a rush. He reached up and pushed her hat back from her head. Her unruly curls fell free, cascading around her shoulders and making her look as beautiful as he'd always imagined she would. Her hands curled around his neck, and she stared at him with those beautiful eyes. When their lips met, it was like a breath from paradise. She was the most precious gift he'd ever received, and he thanked God for allowing them to be together. "I love you, Iris."

A single tear spilled over and traced the length of her cheek. "I love you, too, Adam."

A Letter To Our Readers

Dear Reader:

In order that we might better contribute to your reading enjoyment, we would appreciate your taking a few minutes to respond to the following questions. We welcome your comments and read each form and letter we receive. When completed, please return to the following:

Fiction Editor
Heartsong Presents
PO Box 719
Uhrichsville, Ohio 44683

1. Did you enjoy reading *A Bouquet for Iris* by Diane Ashley & Aaron McCarver?
   ❏ Very much! I would like to see more books by this author!
   ❏ Moderately. I would have enjoyed it more if

   _____

   _____

   _____

2. Are you a member of **Heartsong Presents**? ❏ Yes ❏ No
   If no, where did you purchase this book? _____

   _____

3. How would you rate, on a scale from 1 (poor) to 5 (superior), the cover design? _____

4. On a scale from 1 (poor) to 10 (superior), please rate the following elements.

   ____ Heroine   ____ Plot
   ____ Hero   ____ Inspirational theme
   ____ Setting   ____ Secondary characters

5. These characters were special because? _____
_____
_____

6. How has this book inspired your life? _____
_____
_____

7. What settings would you like to see covered in future
   Heartsong Presents books? _____
_____
_____

8. What are some inspirational themes you would like to see
   treated in future books? _____
_____
_____

9. Would you be interested in reading other **Heartsong
   Presents** titles? ❏ Yes ❏ No

10. Please check your age range:
   ❏ Under 18   ❏ 18-24
   ❏ 25-34   ❏ 35-45
   ❏ 46-55   ❏ Over 55

Name _____
Occupation _____
Address _____
City, State, Zip _____
E-mail _____

CORNHUSKER DREAMS

Relive the glory days of
WWII on the Nebraska
home front and watch as
three women's dreams
are rerouted down the
road to love.

Historical, paperback, 368 pages, 5³⁄₁₆" x 8"

———————————————————

Presents

Great Inspirational Romance at a Great Price!

Heartsong Presents books are inspirational romances in
contemporary and historical settings, designed to give you an
enjoyable, spirit-lifting reading experience. You can choose
wonderfully written titles from some of today's best authors like
Wanda E. Brunstetter, Mary Connealy, Susan Page Davis,
Cathy Marie Hake, Joyce Livingston, and many others.

When ordering quantities less than twelve, above titles are $2.97 each.
Not all titles may be available at time of order.

HEARTSONG
PRESENTS

If you love Christian romance…

$10.99

You'll love Heartsong Presents' inspiring and faith-filled romances by today's very best Christian authors…Wanda E. Brunstetter, Mary Connealy, Susan Page Davis, Cathy Marie Hake, and Joyce Livingston, to mention a few!

When you join Heartsong Presents, you'll enjoy four brand-new, mass-market, 176-page books—two contemporary and two historical—that will build you up in your faith when you discover God's role in every relationship you read about!

Mass Market 176 Pages

Imagine…four new romances every four weeks—with men and women like you who long to meet the one God has chosen as the love of their lives…all for the low price of $10.99 postpaid.

To join, simply visit www.heartsong presents.com or complete the coupon below and mail it to the address provided.

✂ ----------------------------

YES! Sign me up for Heartsong!

NEW MEMBERSHIPS WILL BE SHIPPED IMMEDIATELY!
Send no money now. We'll bill you only $10.99 postpaid with your first shipment of four books. Or for faster action, call 1-740-922-7280.

NAME _____

ADDRESS_____

CITY_____ STATE _____ ZIP _____

MAIL TO: HEARTSONG PRESENTS, P.O. Box 721, Uhrichsville, Ohio 44683
or sign up at **WWW.HEARTSONGPRESENTS.COM**